The Writers of Lovedean

2018 Anthology

The Stories What I Wrote

Table of Contents

Barbara Anders — 1

- July 23rd — 2
- Saffie — 3
- The Sins of the Flesh — 4

Bruce Parry — 13

- Dust — 14
- Pylon — 15
- Sacred Sanctuary — 16
- Silver Threaded Christmas — 18
- Waiting Room White — 19

Christine Lawrence — 23

- The Cherry Orchard — 24
- The Cobbler's Daughter — 26

David Dunford — 28

- Jocasta's Secret — 29
- Lies, Lights and Loneliness — 32
- The Conference of the Entities — 37
- The Owl and the Shapeshifter — 42

David Hudson — 45

- Of Water, Air and Fire — 46
- The Birds of Christmas — 51

Diana Ashman — 54

- Christmas mind dump. — 55
- Free Flight — 56
- Night shift. — 57
- Otto Dix. — 60
- Twilight trees. — 61

Jenny Fisher — 62

GROUPING	63
ALL THE KING' HORSES	67
GAME OF MIRRORS	73
SUMMER HOLIDAY	74
WITCHES BREW	77

Lynne Stone — **81**

BEAUTIFUL LADY	82
SOLD MY SOUL FOR 20P	86
THE NIGHT BEFORE CHRISTMAS	89
THE WALKING STICK	93
WILD THING	96

Margaret Jennings — **99**

IT'S A MYSTERY	100
VENTRI THINGY	102

Mick Cooper — **104**

FOOD GLORIOUS FOOD	105
HEROES	108
HOLY SMOKE	110
JEREMIAH'S MYSTERY	114
TED'S NAKED CONUNDRUM	118

Sheila Brown — **123**

BLACK TULIPS	124
JUNE	126
WHAT A LOAD OF NONSENSE	128

Sue Cornell — **129**

ALL THE KING'S HORSES	130
BOUNDARIES	132
JUNE	134
ON THE THIRD DAY OF CHRISTMAS	137

Sue Maund — **140**

A CHANCE MEETING	141
BERTIE BEE'S NEW JOB	143
BROKEN HEART	146
THE CROC WHO COULD SING	149
THE LION WHO WANTED CURLY HAIR	151
THE TORTOISE WHO THOUGHT HE COULD RACE	153

Barbara Anders

July 23rd

Sunrise announced the dawning
Of another scorching midsummer's day.
Nature's distinctive perfume
Of vintage roses and freshly mown grass
Filled the air.
Sandy, dressed to perfection,
Walked briskly down to his stop
where he occupied his usual seat,
second on the right and waited
For the omnibus to arrive.
Lady Luck revealed her presence.
Sophia arrived and sat beside him.
Two ginger nuts entwined together – total bliss.
Exit paradise.
The bus arrived.
"Where is Ginger Bus, the ginger cat?"
Asked his fans aboard the 21.

Saffie

Golden memories of a memorable lady.
Beauty shone upon her sun-kissed coat.
This gentle giant, fun loving character,
friendly, intelligent,
eager to please Mum Ann.
The adopted mother, companion of galaxy coated Dill.
This life long relationship,
a nudge of her nose, the touch of her paw
administered both comfort and guidance.
Saffie adored woodland walks.
Freedom, the puddle Olympics,
Muddy paws the gold medal reward.
Personal waterfalls exit
the mud in her "Capability Brown" landscaped garden,
and "the green, green grass of home."
Hide and seek a favourite game,
Saffie could often be found hidden,
awaiting a hot Marrigold shower.
Always head of the queue.
A trend setter, the blue boot affair
"First, I don't want this on."
Intelligence resigned for comfort and protection,
Covering a cut pad.
Naturally Dill tried to access this fashion accessory.
Looking down rabbit holes,
a favourite pursuit.
Her Mum's weekly news round with updates of pictorial antics and progress.
Saffie, a beautiful lady remembered.

The Sins of the Flesh

"Tragedy," the Bee Gees recorded this song, the lyrics explain the despair experienced by many intellectuals and students alike, during their academic careers. My story shows how both reality and fiction become interwoven, under the guise of the deadly sins.

Suddenly someone turned the door knob, the door opened, Margarita Zenia Monaveen Wendlesbury slid, like a temptress, into Professor Marcus Landbury's room on the top floor of Queensbury College, Oxbury. The Prof's room had a strange musty smell and eerie atmosphere which sends shivers down your spine when first experienced. Dark wooden panelling surrounded the walls, thousands of volumes filled the shelves of his personal library. His collection of some thirty-five year's work. Dark red velvet curtains shielded the gothic style windows. The Dracula element, where both light "and sunlight were banished into eternity, the moon would turn to blood." The air of death haunted this room with the red mottled carpet, dark heavy looking furniture from gothic times, something sinister is about to occur.

Miss Wendlesbury provided a breath of fresh air, one of the most popular MPhil/DPhil (Doctorate) students. Sophisticated, tall with long raven curly hair cascading down her back, peaches and cream complexion, red luscious lips, smoky eyes, wearing blood like Wok designer spectacles perched on her nose. Dressed in a white long sleeved, crisp cotton shirt, designer clothes, pale blue jeans, the pockets decorated with rhinestones. Covering her slender feet black patent sandals, carrying a black patent Lulu Guinness shoulder bag.

Professor Landbury, distinguished looking, tall, clean shaven with well- manicured hands. Dressed in a white cotton polo neck jumper, blue-black velvet jacket, navy blue trousers and black patent shoes.

When Margarita turned the door knob and entered the room, the professor's blood began to boil, just a glimpse of her affected him like this. He hoped that once her Doctorate had been confirmed he might stand a chance. Marcus was totally besotted with her. Margarita and Marcus meet regularly to discuss both her progress with her Ph.D. Thesis "The attitude to the paranormal in the Victorian novel" and her undergraduate teaching.

Margarita also taught on the World Wide under-graduate 3rd year literature course which meet regularly on Tuesdays and Wednesdays.

Marcus insisted in sitting in on all her seminar lectures, which seemed a little odd to a number of her students. Why would he do this? Would this count towards her Ph.D.? They all suspected he had an ulterior motive. After supervising the last lecture in May, Margarita and her tutorial group had agreed to meet at the Oxbury Union for a pre-graduation Silver Service dinner to celebrate not only the end of term but the end of 3 years of hard work of 'blood, sweat and tears', achieving their individual potential.

Professor Marcus Landbury had other ideas, formal invitations had been sent out to all seminar students, but only one on this occasion for a formal cocktail party in his private rooms. Margarita arrived for her private tutorial at 19:00 hours expecting the cocktail party to follow at 20:00 hours, the invitation had said 19:30 for 20:00 hours. Alarm bells began to ring once Miss Wendlesbury had opened the door, her eyes focused on the table set for dinner for two. Marcus probably had arranged an intimate private dinner party, whilst the students were dining at the Oxbury Union.

Unaware until it was too late, Margarita realised the intended intimate dinner for two had been arranged especially for her. Marcus, the bird of prey, (Dracula), she would be the victim, the draconian mantis web now closing in on her.

This evening Marcus's mood was an extremely relaxed one, Margarita had never seen him so at ease. Landbury's usual manner, that of the stiff upper lip. I am the professor, you are my pupil – the student, the master. This evening Marcus wore a burgundy smoking jacket, cravat, black evening trousers and patent evening shoes, which reminded Margarita of Bram Stoker's "Dracula".

Now she realised exactly what the smells and atmosphere related to, the candelabra, dark red baize tablecloth covered with a lace tablecloth. Would she become one of Dracula's victims? Marcus, apparently, a member of the College Draculians, with a more than healthy interest in this fictional character.

Margarita, seated at the table, enjoying a glass of claret from Marcus's huge wine cellar, renowned for his personal knowledge of wines and with a reputation as importer. The meal uneventful, the food exquisite, they had dined on a remarkable clear soup, a Victorian pheasant dish with fresh seasonal vegetables. The dessert, Margarita thought, warranted the title 'to die for', a meringue basket filled with fresh fruit in a liqueur sauce.

They retired to the Chesterfield dark leather suite. Marcus moved closer to Margarita, and slid his arm round her shoulders, she never even flinched. This could be the perfect end to their liaison of some seven years, and Marcus's alternative motive. The after dinner conversation commenced with a discussion of her thesis and her undergraduate teaching programme success. Sophia, Margarita's friend, would make a good Masters English Literature student, heading for a Ph.D. place if her performance continued to excel, a First with distinction for her B.A. Hons. Degree in English Literature now unquestionable.

'Margarita, you look magnificent tonight,' said Marcus.

'This retro look becomes you,' said Margarita to Marcus.

Margarita, tonight, wore a Grecian style white maxi length figure hugging dress which left little to the imagination. The temptress who had slid into Dr. Marcus Landbury's office would, ultimately, seduce Marcus, the praying mantis about to revenge her prey. Battle plans had been drawn, determined to seduce him, his ulterior motive equalled a tournament of game, set and match. Their feelings were mutual towards each other. Although both had been drinking heavily, their next step would be inevitable, canoodling and enjoying intimate knowledge of each other. Margarita had arrived at seven, the black bird of time had flown by.

The evening was hot and humid, a thunderstorm about to strike. Suddenly Marcus stood up and left the room for a moment, returning with a bottle of vintage champagne and two crystal glasses, they sat sipping champagne – this signified the end. Moving behind her and heading towards the windows to look out into the courtyard below, heavily lit with lights. Student revellers were celebrating. Moving forward towards her, Marcus kissed her on the cheek as Margarita rose to her feet and he kissed her passionately.

At that moment Marcus clasped his hands round her neck and sank his teeth into her swanlike lily white neck as the first clap of thunder together with sheet lightning struck. The whole room had lit up. Margarita fell to the ground, checking for a pulse, evidence of life now extinct. The seducer and superior in rank, the seducer not the praying mantis.

What had he done? His soul mate laying on the floor lifeless; regretting this action he sobbed bitterly. Life without Margarita, his soul mate, together, literally, "the world could have been their oyster."

When the storm had passed Marcus quickly showered and changed, by now it was three o'clock in the morning. The student revellers were either sleeping off the parties or indulging in other carnal pursuits. Quickly and carefully Marcus rolled the body up into the rug. By now sobered up with gallons of water and black coffee, silently he moved his car towards the back entrance, and using the back stairs and lift, removed the body, placing Margarita in the boot of his car. He drove out to the river Y.

Finding a secluded spot, removed the body from the boot of his car, placed Margarita in the river.

'Goodbye my love' he had said.

The body immediately sank, hopefully it would be days or preferably months before the body would be discovered. All traces of his DNA would be removed, the body being partly decomposed.

As Marcus returned to his rooms the dawn chorus announced the start of a beautiful June morning; which echoed the hymn

"Morning has broken." Listening to Beethoven's 5th Symphony, Professor Landbury sat with a heavy heart, his face buried in his hands. Only fear and despair greeted him. Remorse had now set in, with rigor-mortis for Margarita, her watery grave, the River Y.

Within an hour of Margarita's seminar, he came to his senses. What if her body was found? His best plan would be quickly to shower, change and attend her seminar group as usual. Her students would only be suspicious if any dramatic changes took place.

Looking like what could only be described as "worse for wear" or " the morning after the night before", Marcus appeared as usual and waited for Margarita, who today would be "fashionably late", her exact whereabouts known only to him. After her no show, Marcus decided the company should adjourn to the Coffee Hub for an informal social gathering.

Sophia bought the first round, seven cups of delicious Arabian full roast black coffees. They were all suffering in some way, from the fall out of the night before, Marcus was no exception. During the course of the conversation, he revealed that he had dined with friends and mixed his drinks. They all thought that at his age he should have known better. Little did they know this had been an intimate dinner followed by a committal to a watery grave. The conversation moved towards a discussion of the 7 deadly sins, and their relevance today, as we approach the end of the first quarter of the twenty- first century.

The discussion resulted in inconclusive evidence, there were arguments for and against. Religious groups have a very different perspective on life and in the Michaelmas term this would be debated at Oxbury Union, concluding from a general student view point, consciously or unconsciously, all students are guilty of at least one.

Sophia observed Marcus's face when each were discussed in turn. Lust guilty since he first set eyes on Margarita, a lying tongue, he would commit his offence shortly. The ten commandments not discussed during this discussion, also applied to him. "Thou shalt not kill", murder had been committed. Landbury was guilty beyond any shadow of doubt, his DNA would convict him, moreover Geoffrey Chaucer's "The Pardoner's Tale" which is a sermon on the seven deadly sins. Marcus studied this text as an undergraduate.

Sophia watched Marcus, he wondered if she suspected him? Sophia's dissertation entitled "Literary signals", whose research skills were first class and her observant observations excellent. A week passed and there were still no sign of Margarita, enquiries had been made to no avail. Seminar Two passed, Marcus took control, but when asked if he knew the current whereabouts of Margarita his upper lip quivered slightly. Sophia, now concerned for her friend's safety, reported her missing and made an appearance on "Crimewatch."

Marcus had said Margarita had probably returned to London. She had been known to disappear from time to time and become totally immersed working on her new book. This was June and she never missed the Oxbury Union end of academic year party, this was totally out of her character. It was now three weeks since her last communication with Sophia, not only was Margarite her dissertation consultant supervisor (as Marcus is Margarita's dissertation supervisor) but a close and personal friend – they were cousins.

Dr. Marcus Landbury had taken control of seminars in Margarita's absence. Sophia constantly asked Marcus if he had seen or heard from her. The reply was always the same. 'No, Sophia', the deadly sin committed and always with an evil smile and quivering upper lip.

'Margarita may have needed some personal time and space, or even having a secret liaison, which must remain her secret. You're young, you know how life unfolds'.

This was not her style.

Graduation passed and Sophia found it extremely difficult to accept her absence, there was no way Margarita would ever have missed her graduation or the family Mediterranean celebration cruise.

The seasons past. Autumn came and went – the trees lost their leaves. Christmas, the family expected a surprised visit, no card or communication. Obviously, something sinister had occurred. Sophia knew deep down she was dead and had been for some time, possibly since June. Marcus was guilty, and he knew she knew he was the murderer. They watched each other's moves, giving no further signals. Sophia feared for her life, and avoided being alone with him, choosing public places for M.A. tutorials.

By May their secret hostility ceased to be a problem. Margarita had gone, whether voluntarily or involuntarily, each called a silent truce. Sophia graduated with an M.A. in World Classical Literature, next year she would follow in her cousin's footsteps and commence her Ph.D. studies with Dr. Marcus Landbury as her mentor and supervisor.

Michaelmas term started a little later that year. Sophia concentrated on her studies, but Marcus began to notice her in an unprofessional way, leering at her, and maybe snapping her from his window whilst walking across the quadrangle.

Would she be Margarita's replacement? Sophia was the same height and build. The distinguishing feature, her individuality – the natural blonde. This would not stop him, if he wanted to seduce her he would attempt to. Sophia knew how to handle herself in difficult situations. College policy insisted all freshers are required to attend a 6 week self- awareness and defence course.

Marcus continued to make unwanted advances to her, which she recorded in a secret diary, should evidence be required for police prosecution.

Eight years passed with little evidence to support the Magarita case, until her last tutorial before her graduation as Ph.D. in English Literature. Marcus invited her to dinner and cooked a fantastic meal, soup, pheasant, and his famous reputation fruits of the forest liqueur meringue baskets. This mirrored Margarita's last evening of life on this earth.

Again, the night was hot and humid, a thunderstorm and claps of thunder roared in the distance. Sophia, dressed in a red figure hugging dress, which left little to the imagination, silver diamante high heeled sandals. Marcus put his arm round her whilst they were relaxing between courses and attempted to seduce her, both again had been drinking heavily and the inevitable happened. Leaving the room for a moment, returning with two crystal champagne glasses and a vintage bottle of champagne. The creature of habit, suddenly to her immense surprise, went down on one knee and proposed to her. Sophia accepted his proposal of marriage and a huge solitaire rock as she preferred to call the ring. Did she really love him? Her cousin's case of missing person remained open with inconclusive evidence.

Immediately after the graduation Professor Landbury left for the World Wide Lecture of the prestige Universities which was due to commence.

As Sophia walked at dusk along the bank of the River Y she screamed, there appeared to be a metal coffin with the body part of a young woman peeking out. Students hearing her screams came to her assistance, the police were called, the body taken to the mortuary for the post mortem examination. Due to the fact that the body had been concealed in a metal watertight coffin Margarita's family and dental records were able to identify the body.

At the precise moment that Sophia screamed, a Virgin Atlantic aircraft roared overhead, muffled her first screams. The stewardess asked Professor Marcus Landbury if he would like a drink to which he replied 'Yes, I'll have a Bloody Mary please' and sank back into his seat.

Could this be Dracula? – he was only a fictional character in Bram Stoker's novel "Dracula". Or is this just a crime of passion or something more sinister I ask?

Oxbury became a crime scene, strangulation with evidence of carnal knowledge. The Coroner's verdict, strangulation with puncture marks on the neck.

Chief Inspector Jamson led the case and all males connected with Oxbury University had been traced and their DNA tested. Witnesses came forward to support the case that Professor Marcus

Landbury was known to all female students and staff alike as a womanizer.

The Y murder case seemed to drag on and on, every day some new evidence appeared, either linking or eliminating suspects from their enquiries.

Professor Marcus Landbury was arrested at Gatwick Airport on his arrival from his extended visit to the United States. Further investigations of his university rooms and private flat revealed a memorial shrine to Margarita and two other female students who disappeared suddenly without any trace.

This fifty-six year old man, who worked as a respectable Professor of English at Oxbury University, who would have become a Dean of the English Faculty on his return, had access to thousands of young women, whom he enticed after careful selection over many years.

His last victim, Sophia, had a lucky escape, accepting Marcus's proposal of marriage saved her life. Marcus had chosen her because she reminded him of her cousin, whom he truly loved, and as a serial killer, his mind would not allow him to accept reciprocated love. Psychologists would argue that his problem was seated in his unhappy childhood.

The trial lasted for 6 months and Professor Marcus Landbury is now serving a prison sentence for life, which will mean life in a prison hospital.

Bruce Parry

Dust

The dust settled each day upon the varnished finish, those happy times of melodic movement, that gradually diminished to the sitting room…

A solitary Aspidistra stands unwatered, as curtains fade where the sun peeped through and hovered on the Piano lid that was finally closed…

Where once melody was happy, where the hammers found their strings, telling tales of waltzes that spun around Austrian lakes…

Two candle holders each side, have become the saddened eyes, almost searching for the one who has gone, the one who once played, the one who once loved but put music away inside a dark cupboard…

She is gone from the Piano that stands upright, stands alone, facing an oil painting of Viennese waltzes…where dust fades the image…

The trains left, one by one, from village to town, far away to cold places, emptying their loads that became dust…

In Memory of the Holocaust

Pylon

May came into bloom, suddenly, nodding flowers exchanged their flowing currency…

Church bells chimed across the yellow Rape, and red Poppies bobbed in between…growing their sadness once again…

How could it be so bright? Beyond, a puffy sky met a straight stark sea, a breeze whistled through the wired…Harp like fences…

Pylons marched across the land, clutching their humming cables, relentless and tall…

As if travelling over hill and dale, towards some kind of unknown Armageddon, powering our computers and devices…

We sit silently at the other end, staring at screens, unaware of our decline and loss of control, as we are fed more and more artificial intelligence…

The steel giants tread the landscape, dip into valleys, rise across rivers, buzz over lost woodland and reflect hot sun…

The land is patchwork with wild and tidy colourful days, night folds down and keeps it safe in silhouette, until dawn breaks it free…

May came into bloom, suddenly, and was bright, wild deer jumped over hedgerows and gathered in woodland that was magical again…

Sacred Sanctuary

The wind, the rain and snow will arrive, and where will the shelter be…?

Crossing a sea, a sea that engulfs, a new sea that cannot be parted by Moses this time...

Boats of sticks and rubber, planks and cork, man their tormenter again and again…

Slumping onto beaches of Greek tourist tan, lilo dripped ice cream, stuffed vine leaves and the litter of humanity…

A Europe to tread, a tearful release, out of the water, out of danger, heading north…

The new Exodus has begun, the wind, the rain and the snow will arrive, and where will the shelter be…?

I had a dream, could it be possible for all of our western religions to make the ultimate sacrifice…?

Could it be possible for all the churches, in all the countries, in all the cities, in all the towns, in all the villages to open their hearts and doors to house the thousands…?

These giant monoliths to the faithful, giving refuge, giving sanctuary to the needy, the lost, the homeless…

A thousand churches in a thousand places, waiting for the wind, the rain and the snow to come, and where will the shelter be...?

Will the polished pews be beds, will the crypts be kitchens, will the candles bring light to a lost generation, now found…?

The coloured lead light windows will peep out through the snowfall, and reflect across the cemeteries of white…

Will the dead rise up and despise the living, protest at this abomination and intrusion of new arrivals…?

No, they will lay quietly in state, as all the churches in all the countries, in all the cities, in all the towns, in all the villages carry out Gods work, the work everyone wanted God to do…or did we…?

Babbling strange languages will echo through the knave, through the arches and wood, the cold stone no longer hollow…

The wind, the rain and the snow will come, and children's toys will scatter across marble floors, while huddled mothers watch…

While villagers and townspeople bring clothes, blankets, soup and supplies, and refugees will smile and be warm…

Golden crosses, goblets and paraphernalia have no value here, whilst a Syrian woman holds up a ten pence piece, in awe of the Queens head on one side, in a country where a female monarch rules, a Queen, a good Queen, a woman…!

Classrooms will be set up, with Bishops and Saints buried below the scraping chairs and scuffling feet, the honoured dead who will not know these times…

Stand pipes by tombstones will quench the war weary, war torn, sacred sanctuary for a mass displaced…

The wind, the rain and the snows will fall on leaded roof, crystallised steeple, flint and brick, and crying trees…

And so they arrive, into our ancient ark structures, older than this war, older than wars we remember or have forgotten…

The Synagogue's, the Mosque's, the Catholic, the Brethren and Latter Day Saints will fill to the brim these endangered races and cultures, imagine…?

I had a dream, that the wind, the rain and snows will surely fall, across the European Union, over all the churches, in all the villages, in all the towns, in all the cities, in all the countries, places of Sacred Sanctuary…

Still they come, along the trodden miles, rucksacks and prams, out of the water, out of danger, heading north, and where will the shelter be…?

Silver Threaded Christmas

Our fathers, mothers and grandmothers know about Christmas…
Silver threaded hair that matched the weaving of tinsel…
Reflected by the lanterns and bulbs that light the baubles…
On a tree of Christmas past…Christmas charm…
Paper concertina decorations that hang down close…
And touch the Huntley and Palmers biscuit tin and the Young Wireless Operator set, next to a platinum haired doll…
The traipsing of shops and market shout, in the rain, and home with bits of Christmas…
Saving coal for hearty fires, and threading chocolate money with needle darning cotton…
Stocking filling and wrapping that we do not see, tired nights and sleepless sellotape…
The magic pudding that somehow got made, secret and muslin wound, planned from February chill…
Silver threaded with shiny threepenny bits, long before our Christmas morning wake…
Our fathers, mothers and grandmothers know about Christmas, soon arriving and chocolate box tidy…
Those lists they make that we cannot contemplate, item by item, crossed off in the advent countdown…
Years that fly…years that take…years that mark our growing and changing Christmas wishes...
The fathers, mothers, grandmothers and granddads are gone now, merged into Christmas past…
We are Christmas now, fathers, mothers, grandmothers and granddads, knowing about Christmas…
Silver threaded hair that matches the weaving of tinsel, reflected by the lanterns and bulbs that light the baubles…
On a tree of Christmas past…Christmas charm…

Waiting Room White

My late mother said to me one day, "everyone I know is dying around me", she was going through her large address book crossing out another name, address and Birthday. "There's two gone this month she said, I've known them since 1962, this is when you really do start feeling old she said, the old and the famous people who I idolised and who have always been there are disappearing one by one." This went quite deep with me at the time and after mum died, I went through her address book looking at the crossed off friends and relatives one by one, and the year they left, the white haired, the wheelchair bound, the ones that never replied, the old that became older and disappeared from smart houses, the ones that never travelled, the aunts we knew and then didn't know as all of our lives became more disconnected and oh so far away.

I noted the ticks for each year a Christmas card was sent, a birthday card, a condolence card, and I thought about how Mail travelled backwards and forwards, year by year, posted in a hurry, in the rain or from a car when life was good, different stamps and air mail to places beyond our understanding. Yes indeed, this address book was truly a book of the dead, once upon a time, having so much meaning and thoughtfulness, its pages now dog eared and kitchen spill tainted, and where different coloured pens ran out at the wrong time, from black biro start, to red biro finish.

Years have passed, I still have the address book, kept as a reminder of those days, but today, I sit in a hospital waiting room, the audiology and hearing clinic, it's heaving and it's a busy day today, a sea of white heads where I am now included, thinking about mum's address book, everyone here could be the contents of that book, getting closer to being crossed off, being forgotten.

Today's waiting room was much like many others throughout the hospital, the walking frames with wheels, the frames without, the electric disability cart sporting flags for Merrie England and the George Cross football fanatic. The hearing aids in one ear, a broken one in the other, packs of batteries distributed ad lib, packs of old batteries being dumped in the recycle bin, announcing, "dispose of your old batteries here!"

The battery disposal bin sports a cartoon of a giant smiling battery, with arms and legs, "recycle here" in cartoon words with thumbs up that everyone is doing their bit for battery and country, some people were smiling at this, perhaps the only thing they would smile at today!

All of us are fiddling and nervously rolling our next number 'turn' tickets, pulled out of a machine that was originally fixed to the wall, but now lies on the reception counter exhausted from coming away from the wall so many times, maintenance has finally given up on it. Now, all of us are hoping someone will leave so that we can move up the queue faster, get out of here, it's too hot anyway, the heating is up full in case somebody dies of cold, from coming in from the outside Spring warmth, jobs worth health and safety is at a premium in here and there is no escape this time!

The range of walking sticks is greatly varied today, the old fashioned wooden sticks with out of proportion rubber feet that almost stick to the worn floor, the fancy dandy aluminium sticks with double handles and a built in l.e.d. torch that would put a WW2 searchlight to shame. Double stick patients that have had years of practice, who now command veteran status and adoration from an almost envious crowd watching such skill and versatility.

I'm feeling very much alone here today, most people are ten years my senior but I sit and look at my possible future, thinking about mum's address book, thinking about everyone here, I can see their past lives, the bright sunshine of front garden tended Roses, skipping pavements, recreation grounds, hedge trimming and ladders against houses to paint a perfect world brighter. The quiet tide of Sunday morning church bells in all of their towns, those reassuring bells of innocent childhood, quiet streets and corner shops, that Sunday morning peace that closed noisy factories and offices, streaky bacon waft and joint in the oven, telling of an optimistic future when we were still nice.

I'm looking across to a lady slightly bent over, leaning on her old wooden walking stick that has done the miles, has seen life and guided her over tripping pavements and slipping wet leaves. I bet she makes apple pies, dotted with cloves, was she an absolute stunner in her twenties, did she I wonder, trap her late husband with sex on the beach, or in the sand dunes, maybe she was more of an under the Pier girl, followed by a lifetime of apple pies that stood the test of time. She sits alone staring at the cartoon of the giant battery with arms and legs, and does not smile.

I pick up 'Bright Life, Easy Life' mail order catalogue from the magazine pile, flicking through it dawns on me that this is what it's come to, a twilight zone of mail order products for a long living declining generation. A light up owl with integral spring, that spins the head round and screeches at unwanted cats in a twelve foot square pebbled garden. A wire rack that stores multiple tinned food cans sideways, but you can't see what tins they are at the back, ideal for a nuclear fallout situation. A leaf blowing machine that blows leaves in all directions, but never clears them up and piles them in banks. A long reach bug vac that lets you suck up creepy crawlies from a safe distance. Shoes that are so comfortable that they could be slippers, but they really are shoes, but they look like slippers, lovely for a walk up the local co-op! "These are surely glamorous days!"

I strike up conversation with an increasingly agitated man sat next to me, his ticket is now folded up at least eight times and it has become an unrecognisable tiny square in his hand. "It's never been this busy he said, people are now standing room only and nobody knows who to give their seat up to", I agreed, saying "that perhaps a walk in clinic was not such a good thing, he couldn't hear a word I said!" A nurse quickly rescued us by going round trying to prioritise the lesser audio repairs as compared to the more complex issues, bringing in more staff for the simpler repairs seemed to do the trick.

So here we are, all alone in our separate bubbles, edging towards the next number to be called, not knowing when our number is up, the giant smiling battery recycle bin with arms and legs grins back at our hopeless attempts at longevity, like a giant cynical Humpty Dumpty who knows, that "All the kings horses and all the kings men could never put us back together again."

Christine Lawrence

The Cherry Orchard

When I'm lying on my back with my arms in stirrups to stop me from moving so that they can fire the radiotherapy waves at my left breast, I look up at the screen on the ceiling above my head. It's a photograph of a cherry tree in blossom with the light behind it. The picture has been taken from below with the blue sky in the background so that you can imagine that you really are in a Cherry Orchard.

I can feel the slightly damp grass beneath me and sense the cool breeze bringing relief from the heat of the day. There's hardly a cloud in the sky - just the sound of a nearby bee and the blackbird who's hiding in the higher branches. I am six years old again and have nothing to do but lie in the long grass, look up at the tree and dream of the future yet to come.

For many years, throughout most of my adulthood in fact, I have longed to lie on the grass and just gaze up at the sky through branches such as these, laden with white blossom, just to watch the changing shapes of the clouds and to think about nothing.

Now, at last I have time to lie here and look up. But the sky isn't alive, the clouds are set in the same formation as they were yesterday. The blossoms don't quiver in the breeze - there is no breeze. It's just a photograph, there to take your mind off the radio-waves that they're firing at you.

This is just a moment in time, I think, and try not to start wondering how I could have got to this point. Me, who was so ordinary, sailing through life convinced that cancer was for fools and I was not a fool. Now though, I am living in a bubble, caccooned against real life, with a cancer label floating like a balloon on a string, high above my head. You can't forget it's there. When you go through a doorway, sometimes the balloon gets caught but it soon bounces through and entangles in your hair like the wind on a stormy day.

I lie and look through the snowy blossoms and notice that tears are leaking from my eyes. Don't move, I'm told, so I am still and try not to mind the little river which runs down the sides of my face and into my ears. I focus on the sky and promise myself that as soon as summer comes I will take time to lie under the Cherry tree in my garden.

Soon this phase in my life will be over, then I'll look back on it and smile. I will hold the string of the balloon in my hand one last time and finally let it go. I'll make sure that the wind is in the right direction and doesn't get caught up in the branches of the tree. I will laugh out loud and be happy.

The Cobbler's Daughter

It's so cold and dark - the darkness competing with the cold to penetrate my very bones. My hands are numb and can't feel the buttons on my boots as I fumble to dress myself. Hurry! Hurry! I panic as I tumble down the attic stairs trying in vain to make no noise as I fall.

I run through the welcome warmth of the vast kitchen - breathe in the aromas of delights Iwill never have in my belly - into the damp chill of the scullery - my domain.

'You're late,' snaps Betty, the under-parlour maid. I know she's got it in for me. I duck my head out of her reach but she hasn't taken a swipe at me this time.

I quickly gather up my tools in the wooden bucket and stagger back up the stairs to the main entrance hall. I stand for a moment and can feel the silence of the house - still in darkness - just the ticking of the grandfather clock a heartbeat of the centre of this monster I live in.

Shaking myself into action I start the day's work of cleaning the fireplaces and lighting the fires. A warm feeling of anticipation of what the day may bring seeps through me. Today is special - my half day off. As soon as I've finished my work here I can take the afternoon off - just as long as I'm back by six o'clock to scrub the floors below stairs before going to bed. Head down, I work hard at my polishing, keen to get away before three.

At last it's time to go. Peeling off my cap and apron I don my black bonnet and cape, slip from the kitchen and soon I'm walking down the black path that leads to the village. As I pass the church I hear the sound of pigs squealing from the back yard of the Post Office opposite the church. Mr. Faithful must be slaughtering again - fresh pork for sale tomorrow!

I walk on down West Street until I reach our home, a low thatched cottage with tiny dormer windows. Through the side gate and down the garden path - I make straight for the workshop. As I enter my father looks up from his work - a leather shoe in one hand, a hammer in the other. The smell of leather and glue fills the air - a lovely homely smell. His eyes light up when he sees me but I can see behind the light a troubled shadow. We exchange greetings - I kiss him fondly on the cheek.

'What's the matter?' I ask.

'I've blotted me copybook with the squire,' he replies. 'He came in here with a pair of boots needing mending and wanted 'em done by Sunday afternoon. Well, you know I never work on the Sabbath so I told him they won't be ready until Monday. Well he had no choice, being as his regular cobbler is in London and it would take twice as long to get 'em there and back. Then whenhe comes to collect them I told him the cost was half a crown. He didn't like that - said he could get 'em done in London for two shillings. So I says "take 'em to London then!"

'He went off in a foul mood at that and today I gets this letter from the agent telling me my tenancy's terminated - with seven days notice! After three hundred years of my family living here! I can't fathom it.'

I can hardly believe it either and we spend time talking in circles - trying to work out what we can do about it. How can someone who calls himself a Christian put out a man who's worked and lived all his life here - he who was crippled when he was a small boy working in the Squire's wood mill.

Two hours later I begin the walk back to the House - my heart heavy. There's nothing to be done, I know. Father will have to move out and there's nowhere to go. All our family are dead but me. Father says at least I have a roof over my head and he'll be alright whatever happens. I know what that may be - the only thing left for him - take himself to the Workhouse. There at least he'll have food and shelter and with his skills as a cobbler he should be able to survive.

Will I ever see him again?

David Dunford

Jocasta's Secret

Pat ordered 2 J2O's and sat at a table facing the window knowing Margaret would be along soon and have the same. Sure enough she joined her a couple of minutes later. Two sisters, two years apart and like peas in a pod. Both tall and slender with brunette hair in the same bobbed style, smoky blue eyes behind similar glasses and identical dimpled cheeks. It was their first catch up since their mum had died and they waited eagerly for their third sister to arrive.

The Range Rover stopped at the entrance, a short well-built, expensively dressed woman stepped out and the car drove off. The woman oozed wealth and success. They both watched as she approached the door, Margaret noticed a slight shake of Pat's head and knew what she was thinking.

"Makes you wonder every time doesn't it, and now Mum's gone we'll probably never know"

"She can't be our sister, she's different from us in every way, not just looks. Neither of us drink but she'll be out of it by the end of the meal. She hates kids but loves material things whereas we're the opposite. Even her names wrong, we've both got traditional names, where the hell does Jocasta come from" Said Pat.

"There's her middle name too, she's never let on, all we ever get is it begins with C"

"That's always bugged you hasn't it, quiet, here she comes"

"Hello girls, sorry I'm late, traffic"

Hugs and air kisses all round, Jocasta ordered a large G&T. Ten minutes later she ordered another, the two girls refused, continuing to nurse their J2O's. The meal consisted of two light lunches of fish and salad with Jocasta ordering Angus beef burger, chips and extra salsa sauce. Both girls noticed she was noticeably less talkative than usual throughout the meal. The excited talk amongst the other two of hubbies, holidays, hairdo's and houses soon gave way to talk of their Mum and how they missed her.

Silence descended and they all started thinking separate thoughts, eventually Margaret broke the silence and spoke to Pat.

"How did your mammogram go?"

"Oh! Clean bill of health, go again in five years"

The G&T's let her down and Jocasta muttered "Lucky you" instantly regretting it.

Two sets of eyes immediately on her "Jo?"

A brief beat of silence, a deep breath, then a sigh

"Oh you may as well know, I went some time ago. I have a small lump they're going to take out but I also had the other tests. I have the gene. There's a 40% chance of it coming back before I'm 55 and an 80% chance of me getting it in later life". She said it in the deadpan way of people who have kept a secret for a long time. The other two stared back at her.

"What do you mean, you have the gene?"

"I inherited it"

"But if you inherited it, we ought to be tested."

Jocasta picked her words carefully. "That won't be necessary, strange as it may seem I inherited it from my dad"

"But..." Pat stopped herself just in time.

"Oh come on I know you've both suspected it for years, Dad wasn't my biological dad, mum never let on to him and he died not knowing. She was furious when my real dad told me, and he only did that to bathe in my success. But in truth I've always known I was different from you two.

Margaret this time. "You knew before Dad died"

"Oh yes. I've known for years."

Pat could contain herself no longer. "Who was it?"

Jo studied the floor. "Quentin Fortesque Fforbes"

"What! Mum and Dad's boss! That pompous twit who owned the factory where they worked?

Jo nodded.

"But why did Mum..." said Pat

"How do you think she got that job as his PA. She had no qualifications. It wasn't easy bringing us three up back then remember, and we wanted for nothing."

Pat put her hand over her mouth. "Oh Jo"

"It's alright"

Margaret was still taking it all in. "Dad hated him. He used to come round home every Christmas with a hamper"

"Yes," said Jo. "Usually when dad was out if you remember. Mum used to pack us off upstairs and sit in the kitchen with him so we couldn't hear."

Long forgotten memories were coming together. "Oh Jo" Said Pat again.

The silence lingered, Jo ordered another G&T, the others again refused, each with their own thoughts.

It was Margaret who eventually spoke. "Always insisted on getting his own way he did, never listened to anyone else. What with that and his warped sense of humour"

"You're right there on both counts" said Jo

"What do you mean?

Jo looked resigned.

"Well, he agreed I could have our surname because it obviously suited him, but he insisted, and I mean insisted, on my other two names, including my middle one, which as you know, I never use. You two are the only ones who even know it begins with a C.

They both looked expectantly at her.

"Can't you guess?"

The two girls gave identical shakes of their heads.

"Cuckoo"

Lies, Lights and Loneliness

Rowland arrived at the village hall early, he'd waited a long time for this and wasn't going to miss it. A loner who rarely ventured out, this was going to be the highlight of his month. He sat near the back, inconspicuous but with a good view.

A slightly built man took the stage dressed in a poorly fitting camouflage pattern safari suit. It had pockets all over it, each bulging with something, Rowland glimpsed scissors, a multi ink pen and a small torch among others. The notepad incorporated into the trousers just above the right knee added a ludicrous note.

"Stupid nerd". Thought Rowland.

Good Evening and welcome to the Deanbourne Astral Phenomenon Society monthly meeting. If I'm not mistaken I see a few new faces here. So for those who don't know me I'm Trevor Hill and I'm the chairman of the society. We have a busy schedule tonight so without further ado let me hand you over to Belinda Amhurst of Merlin housing management association who is going to talk on 27 Talisman Walk, an empty house with a somewhat shady past.

"What shady past?" thought Rowland hiding a smile, "I know I actually live over the road but I've rented it for over thirty years"

Belinda had not wanted to do the presentation, she was much more at home in her real job but she bravely climbed the steps to the stage, stood in front of the projector and immediately started to squint, Trevor immediately got back on stage and, in what he thought was a gracious manner, escorted her to the lectern, leaving the stage with a patronising smile to the audience.

She had practised hard and started well.

"Myself and Mr Hill conducted our survey of 27 Talisman Walk in the first week of October at the request of four of the Deanbourne Astral Phenomenon Society members and anonymous telephone calls from three anxious members of the public.

"Anxious, my arse" thought Rowland "mind you I'd practised that sob and stutter routine for weeks, leaving messages on the answerphone so I could listen to them when I got home. I wonder who the other two were though, I knew that weirdo down the job centre would fall for it, and that silly mare I met online, but the others... Just goes to show, people really want to believe this stuff."

Belinda pushed on. "Here is the first slide." A typical 50's council house showed on the screen. Trevor could not resist another interruption and leapt onto the stage.

"I feel I should point out at this point that although this dwelling looks normal, it is actually very interesting. Not all paranormal phenomena occur in Gothic castles, I do assure you. Thank you Belinda, carry on."

She hid her annoyance.

"It was the night of the full moon and as we approached the house we noticed shadows on the roof. I was told by Mr Hill that they bore a remarkable resemblance to astral signs. We took four photographs of them.

"Looks like shadows from clouds to me" thought Rowland looking at four photographs of shapeless shadows."

Belinda pushed on.

The property is empty and not maintained but rent is paid regularly to the housing association, even though the owner cannot be traced. In spite of the huge housing shortage in this area we cannot put people in it without his permission. Not that anyone wants to live there with its reputation. The neighbours to the property are also requesting relocation and nobody will move in once we have rehoused them making the housing shortage worse.

"Good!" thought Rowland, his spite showing through.

"Only once has a man been seen entering the property."

"Too right, only the once" thought Rowland. "When I had to replace the timers after that power cut. That's sorted now though with the remote app." His face remained impassive as he listened on.

"One of the most disturbing aspects of the house is the noise and the lights, it has been seen a few times now, we even got some footage from a mobile phone"

"I should hope you bloody did" Thought Rowland as a weird metallic hooning filled the room. "Amazing what a computer can do with sound these days. Didn't cost much either, mind you those speakers I put under the floorboards cost a bit, and the app for the remote control. The weird sound stopped but white light continued to flicker randomly across the windows and then stopped.

"Stupid sods missed the best bit" thought Rowland "I should have had the coloured LED's shine on to that little glitter ball first, not the white one. Mind you it was a good idea that ball, battery lasts forever! Good old internet! All the way from China. It fitted next to the speakers a treat and the cracks in the floorboards were just big enough to let the light through, really added to the spooky effect.

Belinda apologised again for not having more film and said that a search of the property had revealed nothing untoward, no sign of forced entry or regular habitation but that Trevor had felt that the house definitely had a sinister astral presence.

"Pillock" thought Rowland feeling pleased with himself. "Mind you I didn't expect them to find anything.

Belinda was finishing up with obvious relief that her ordeal was over.

"And that concludes the talk for tonight ladies and gentlemen, thank you all for your attention." Trevor was immediately back on stage, anxious for the limelight

Thank you Belinda for a most interesting talk. I think what you have described is a manifestation of one of the rarer forms of African black magic, often found in the Eastern regions of that continent in those countries that have a past going back thousands of years, Ethiopia or Sudan probably. I have read widely on this. It definitely warrants further study and I shall be seeking the permission of the housing management association to carry that out.

Rowland knew that the group finished up at the pub after a meeting and he got there before them. A rare frequenter of pubs, he treated himself to a pint and a whisky chaser and sat down reflecting on a job well done.

"Bunch of absolute nutters, all of them, especially that prat in the suit with all the pockets. Put one over 'em a treat. Eastern African Black Magic, what a load of old crap."

At that moment Trevor and Belinda came in with a couple of others and headed straight for the bar, drinks sorted, they looked around for somewhere to sit and headed straight for him. He hadn't anticipated this and suddenly he was surrounded.

"Your first meeting with us wasn't it?" said Trevor,

"Er Yes"

Have you ever seen the house?

"Er No"

"What did you make of the presentation?"

Rowland didn't like crowds and he liked questions even less. He took a long pull of his whisky trying to think of something to say.

"Yes,Yes, very good. Pity you missed the coloured lights". Belinda was immediately alert.

"How did you know there were coloured lights?

Rowland coughed, spluttered and went wide eyed.

"You said so"

"No I didn't." Belinda looked behind him to someone who put a hand on his shoulder

"I thought it was him"

It showed on Rowlands face, he couldn't think, panic was coming on. Trevor produced a warrant card from one of his many pockets.

Rowland Barratt, I am arresting you…

****

Rowland went to the station in the back of a police van, bemused at the speed of it all. Belinda and Trevor travelled in an unmarked police car.

"It was good of the real Astral society members to keep quiet." said Belinda

"Yeah they're alright, no harm to anybody. But he's a vindictive sad little loner, and they're dangerous". Said Trevor, "Empty life, nothing to keep him occupied. Still wonders what's hit him."

"I could have hit you when you kept jumping on stage. And where did you get that ridiculous get up?"

"What do you mean?" Borrowed it off the real Astral society chairman.

The Conference of the Entities

The seven life forms consisted of pure energy and met in a universe where no other life existed. By using senses incomprehensible to man they conversed, each releasing energy to a central point where it was picked up by the others.

"It's on the Inner rim of the Orion Arm of the Milky Way. A yellow dwarf sun but the third planet contains life forms that are quite remarkable" said Entity One

"Yes, I know of them, some of us have had dealings before." said Entity Four, "A carbon based bipedal life form, they are capable of considerable intelligence, but are they not still extremely violent to one another? They must overcome that before any advancement is considered"

Entities Two, Three and Seven sent bursts of energy signifying their agreement.

"I too know of this race, having spent time observing them." said Entity Five. "At times they have come close to observing us, particularly at this time of year. This occurs because of a weakness in the fabric of space time there and they unknowingly exploit it. Their domesticated animals also notice it and that forewarns them. We need to be extra vigilant because they practise it all over their world giving the event many different names, Halloween and Walpurgis Eve for example."

"Yes their many languages are a mixed blessing to them

"They are also getting their heads around quantum theory and the concept of multiverses." Said Entity Six. "This is a worry even though polyverses are still beyond them.

"So I believe." Said Four. "Apparently they usually justify their sightings of us with religious, mystical or mythological rationales, rarely applying scientific logic, which is unusual for them. Before long they will realise that to use their own phrase, there is something out there."

What would pass as laughter on Earth rippled across all seven beings.

Entity One brought the meeting back to order with a wave of cold energy that made the rest listen.

"We must remember that a lot of the violence they practise on one another is of our making. Whilst the Jesus manifestation is considered a success it created schisms and splinter groups that still fight today"

"Yes and the Hitler manifestation more recently was a disaster." Said Entity Two.

"We have been much more successful when instead of sending an entity disguised in their form we have pointed a human individual in the right direction. Mendel and his beans led them directly to understanding DNA and they have made many medical advances as a result." Said Entity Four

"You could also say it led to eugenics, the holocaust and the failure of the Hitler manifestation." Said Entity Six.

Entity Four tried again.

"We helped Einstein discover the mass energy relationship. He could not have made such an intellectual leap alone and it has had many consequences"

"Some of which led to nuclear bombs, deadly on any planet, especially one that small." Said Six.

Entity Four stayed silent.

No communication passed as the collective intelligence of the seven considered the problem. A human brain the size of Jupiter could not have matched them.

Eventually Entity Five said. "They have increasing problems in obtaining sufficient quantities of both food and energy. With some thought we could beam down more energy which if used correctly would solve both problems."

"What have you in mind?" said One

"They have a single moon that only reflects a small amount of sunlight back to Earth. If we were to increase the reflectivity of the moon's surface we could increase the amount of energy falling on the Earth by 25%." Said Five

"Yes." Said One. "And no direct intervention with anything on the Earth."

"How would you do it? Said Two

"A single nuclear vehicle sent on a spiral trajectory such that it is always hidden from Earth by the moon. "The impact would occur on the farside at a crater site where the moon's mantle is thin and at a speed such that it enters the moon's core and detonates. The heat generated melts the surface making it shiny and more reflective. By tailoring the nuclear isotopes we could ensure reflection increased gradually, taking fifty years or so."

Five's energy radiation profile showed he was pleased with his suggestion and the other Entities were obviously impressed.

"How long would the effect then last?" asked Three

"Oh at least 50,000 years. Then the moons mass would then degrade affecting its orbit around the Earth. We could deal with it then."

"What have we done like this before" asked Four

"Nothing on such a small scale but the ignition of the supernova at the Crab nebula was initiated by us and is similar. That is still providing energy for the beings on the Pan Janneranic system. They have now populated over half of their nearby planets.

The Entities silently considered. Then Entity One spoke

"Consensus?" he asked and six waves of agreement radiated across the whole of the universe.

"Yours to do Five" said One.

******

"Just my luck to be on shift at Halloween." said the technician at the Royal Greenwich Observatory as he started his evening shift. Two hours later he recalibrated his lunar seismograph twice before calling everybody on the emergency wake up list. His screens showed the moon ringing like a bell but, to everybody's relief, remaining in stable orbit. It was reported in the Press as a moonquake and generated little interest because no one had died. Two years later scientists reported to their political masters that there were temperature changes on the moon's surface but it was another year before the Prime Minister, forced to react because the changes would soon become visible, informed the public in a statement that was simultaneously read by every political leader in the world.

"Our scientists have been carefully monitoring this for several months and assure me there is absolutely no danger to the public." They said. "We will, of course, continue to monitor the moon very closely and I pledge to inform the country as soon as I have more information."

Headlines for a week then the story lost its legs. The doom merchants ran out of frightening scenarios and life went on.

When the deserts of Africa and China became habitable people went there in droves often to live beside the new rivers flowing through them. The Australian government, realising it would need people to develop and profit from its vast interior, welcomed anyone who would work.

The overpopulated coastal cities were now beginning to disappear as the ice caps melted, with the loss of a billion people. For the six billion left the Earth was no longer crowded, habitable land was everywhere. The brave and adventurous went to Antarctica and developed hydroponic food systems. They soon made fortunes.

All land on the Equator was unbearably hot and solar energy systems sprang up like weeds, the workers living in vast air conditioned cities, now affordable as energy prices fell dramatically.

Country boundaries ceased to exist as the rivers marking them changed, coastlines did the same and the politicians were helpless to act.

It was a time for 'can do' people and these flourished, often leading large bodies of followers into the Sahara or the higher slopes of mountains where the land was incredibly fertile.

All the while the Entities watched with interest resisting all temptation to interfere.

Some time later Entity Five received a wave of energy from the others.

"Job well done Five" it said.

The Owl and the Shapeshifter

The owl left its nest just after dusk and flew past the castle to its branch in the churchyard. It was his usual perch for hunting mice but tonight he waited, watching but not looking for food. He knew. The moon was full and partially obscured by cloud, but his incredible vision enabled him to watch the faint shadows lengthen.

He missed nothing and he saw it materialise, a grey shape getting darker and forming a human form hovering over the ground

"Shape shifter". He thought as it floated through the gravestones, leaving no trace, making no sound. It stopped above the freshly covered grave as if reading the tributes, the flowers already wilting.

The church clock struck midnight, each toll dying slowly away. The shape appeared to look directly at the owl and then sank slowly into the grave, the flowers never moved but the grave pulsed with an eerie grey light. The owl's keen hearing caught a metallic discordant note as if knives were being scraped together along their sharp edges. It was in perfect sync with the light from the grave.

The woman strode through the lychgate, approached the grave and stopped before it just as the last stroke of midnight died away. She also looked at the owl but it did not return her gaze. Rotating its head through 360 degrees it then gave a single mournful hoot and moved silently along the branch to a darker spot.

The glow from the grave was brighter now but still not lighting the surroundings. The grey shape rose from the grave as silently as it had entered, taking on as it did so an emaciated human image. His voice carried easily on the night air.

"Believe me they will not like this, you're not even in a pentacle"

The woman tossed her head. "You forget I know more about the celestial sphere than you can possibly imagine. I will deal with the Seventh Cohort of Eternal Damnation in due course.

Far away thunder rumbled and flashes lit up the Eastern sky.

"They are coming" said the shape.

"Have you got it?"

A thin bony hand gave the woman a piece of flesh less than an inch in diameter an artery protruded from it, blood showing darkly in the moonlight.

"Complete with blood supply as you requested. Taken from the body just as it left for the Pearly gates. The only time it takes on a physical form."

The woman gazed impassively at it. "A human soul, an actual human soul"

The thunder was definitely closer but the woman was ready. With a silent nanosecond flash she disappeared out of worldly dimensions, beyond time, space and all its manifestations.

The shape shifter never stood a chance, he and the owl were dealt with before the cohort leader landed. People would speculate for years on how the gravestone had appeared at the head of the grave overnight but the shape shifter had to gaze mutely at them entombed in granite until the cohort chose to deal with him. The owl was similarly entombed in the tree, unable to hoot or move but seeing and hearing all. They both gazed at the two figures alongside the grave.

The head of the Seventh cohort had chosen to manifest herself as a large black witch and was surprised to see the Grim Reaper arrive with her, a measure of the seriousness with which they both viewed the situation. The Reaper spoke first, his voice, with its usual perfect tone and diction, coming from the black void inside his hood where a head should normally be.

He addressed the tombstone and looked beyond it to the tree to where the owl was entombed.

"You will both be punished for your respective parts this in due course. But first we will deal with this gross and somewhat serious breach of the fabric of the continuum."

He then turned to the witch.

"How did you get to hear of all this?

"Would you believe from the Archangel Gabriel? Earlier today. First time I'd ever spoken to him"

No one could see the expression on the reapers face but his gasp said it all. After a short pause he said.

"So they knew about it but couldn't stop it?"

"I've said it before, you should never underestimate these humans. Forever probing, forever curious. They never leave anything alone. They were always going to find a way sooner or later."

"Where did she go?"

"Probably out of this universe" he paused considering for a moment,

"But probably not out of our jurisdiction. I have the whole cohort on it"

"Good, keep me posted. I'm sure Gabriel's boss will want to speak to us both about this very shortly"

David Hudson

Of Water, Air and Fire

Back then weekends driving my Mustang, alone, in the foothills was one of life's great joys. But this case arrived on a Tuesday, my squad car had a passenger and the foothills were smouldering.

On arrival the Fire Chief gave me the low down.

"It's beyond bizarre Harry. A corpse in a wet suit."

We headed to the scene. The stench of burnt flesh and charcoal all prevailing. The body was slumped against a tree his rubber trappings melting around him.

"So this is where you found him?"

"Sure, been waiting for you. Never seen nothing like it."

My partner, O'Hara, wiped his streaming eyes and coughed out a question.

"How did he get here?"

The Fire Chief shrugged his shoulders.

"Beats me, there ain't a vehicle in the forest car park. I'd guess he's been here a couple of days, maybe more. Could have died of smoke inhalation. Who knows? Well, gotta go, he's all yours Harry."

We returned to the car and I called the police morgue.

"Yes I can confirm the deceased is in a wetsuit. And there's more, he's still wearing goggles and a snorkel. You're busy. Now I know he's late, but could he jump the queue? I really need an autopsy. Ok you'll do your best."

O'Hara hand me a piece of gum.

"Tricky case boss."

"Yep, any ideas?"

"Well he could have had a fetish."

"Like what?"

"Well maybe he liked walking in the woods in a wet suit."

"O'Hara, tell your parents your expensive education was wasted on you."

"Well boss you did ask me think outside the box."

"Come on O'Hara, let's rope this place off and call in the forensic unit."

I let O'Hara return to base with the fire crew to search out missing persons. It gave me an hour to recce the place. The glade floor was covered in soot but there were no signs of a footprint made by flippers; the diver never walked in the woods. Maybe amongst the footprints were those of a guy who brought him to his resting place. We'd arrived too late.

The next couple of days we twiddled our thumbs and my forefinger yellowed with nicotine till the autopsy report landed on my desk. It wasn't good news.

Our diver was 5'6", 150lbs, no visible tattoos or other markings. The corpse's extremities were badly burnt; no finger prints. Victim died of drowning in fresh water and had a broken neck.

"O'Hara, it's looking like a homicide. Once more you have my permission to think outside the box."

I studied the autopsy more thoroughly but it created more problems than it solved, and no one in missing persons fitted the bill. I phoned the Fire Chief,we need to keep this under wraps, if the papers get hold of this life would be one long press conference and we had no answers.

An hour later, O'Hara knocked on my door with a coffee, a cake and a cockamamie idea.

"Are there any networks in this part of the Sierra Nevada. Places with underground lakes where he might have died with an accomplice who drowned him and broke his neck?"

I must have looked sceptical.

"Well it's an idea boss."

A phone call to Stanford University Geology Department drew a blank. There are no caves in that part of Sierra Nevada. We were back at square one.

"It's beyond bizarre. Never seen nothing like it." The Fire Chief's assessment. He was right. It was the very strangeness of the scene that had fixated me and put me off the scent. The man had drowned. We'd been looking in the wrong place. After a wasted week, our focus turned to those large expanses of fresh water, the lakes.

Dusty from much rummaging O'Hara arrive with a crumbled relief map of the county.

"Well done O'Hara, take the afternoon off but return at 17.00 hours. We're gonna look over every lake with a car park and with luck we'll find some evening fishermen.

The sun was already low as we make our way through the foothills to Owens Lake. Our first destination didn't look promising; an elderly fisherman and an old car parked a hundred yards away.

"Caught anything?"

"Nothing. You a cop?" I gave him a grin and pointed towards the car park.

"You're lucky to get here in that."

"Oh that ain't my car, been here a while, probably dumped."

At last we might have a lead. The car, an old Studebaker, would be easy to trace. There weren't many made before they went bust 25 years ago in 1960. We gave it a brief inspection. The doors were secure, but the cushions on the bench front seat suggested the driver was short and needed help to reach the pedals. The man in the morgue was 5'6". I took the registration and gave forensics a call. It would be interesting to know if there was any trace of a passenger. With luck I'd know its owner by noon tomorrow.

Eating my lunch the next day I was still scratching my head. The garage owner could only confirm the details we already knew, the buyer was a short guy, slim build who didn't give his name. To him it had all been a straightforward transaction; 250 bucks exchanged and nothing suspicious. Forensics called, the car interior was clean, no sign of there being a passenger. In the trunk was a pair of jeans, shoes, a sweatshirt and an empty aqualung. Progress. We could now affirm that the man in the morgue owned the car and had arrived at the lake alone.

I needed to find the old fisherman whose name I hadn't bothered to take.

"Oh Ben, the fisherman's called Ben." O'Hara informed me a little too smug for his own good.

"We exchanged names when I introduced myself."

"Introductions, how very Ivy League of you O'Hara, what else did they teach you at Princeton?"

Dusk, and Ben was lakeside. I let O'Hara quiz him, content to listen.

"Ben did you ever see the driver of the old Studebaker?"

"No, no no-one did."

"How do you know?"

"Cos no one was here, the fish weren't biting, they were too troubled."

"Why were the fish troubled Ben?"

"Cos of the fires."

I was puzzled and intervened.

"Ben, why should a forest fire trouble fish?"

"It ain't the fire exactly, it's the planes that fly low down the valley and scoop up the water before dumping it on the forest. Fish hate roughed up water."

An awful thought crossed my mind and I wasn't alone. After bidding Ben farewell, O'Hara tugged my arm. "The diver, he drowned in mid-air didn't he boss?"

I gave him a nod and replied "Possibly O'Hara, even maybe."

A day of enquiries confirmed that the victim could have been part of the 2,000 gallons collected in the planes' reservoir before it dropped its payload from a height of 300ft. at 200 knots. The diver was already dead before he plummeted into the forest, his neck snapped as he crashed into the trees.

His corpse was never collected, it remains in Stanford Medical Centre's morgue, freshers recoiling as it glides out of the freezer. The case gave me 15 minutes of fame and my face on the front pages of the Los Angeles Times. As for his name well that's a mystery.

The Birds of Christmas

Edvard Janson died on a Sunday, leaving 3 windows of his Advent calendar unopened. He passed away on the remote island he shared with his butler and fellow ornithologist, Mr. Loveless. Robert Alfred Loveless was the sole beneficiary of his will, an unremarkable document save for the deceased's final request.

'Upon my death my limbs are to be dismantled and recycled; the rest of me is to be given to the birds.' Mr. Loveless placed the Philips screwdriver into its slot and taking his fountain pen to the diary gave the 24th a big tick. Outside, the foghorns that plagued the night were muted as the haar mist thickened across the Lofoten Islands and the distant fjord coast. It was time for bed.

Morning, and a visit to the scrapyard. It was deserted. He knew it would be. The two men were the only people on the island in winter. The limbs of the deceased were tossed amongst the mangled marine junk. Minutes later the car arrived at the beach. The pebbles of the shore were separated from the sea by a mile of ice, a "no man's land" patrolled by scavenging petrels and skuas. They honed in on their Christmas dinner; the shaved corpse Mr. Loveless had left them. From the comfort of the car, the ornithologist took notes and observed as they ripped flesh off in great chunks and gorged themselves till replete, they allowed the hovering gulls to finish off the titbits. The pecking order had been observed.

The bare bones were collected and placed in the boot of the car. As requested they would be ground to a fine powder and released on a stormy night. With a fair wind, Edvard Janson's genes would forever haunt the Polar wastes.

Returning home past the scrapyard, the car was brought to a halt. The scavengers of the corpse appeared to be rearranging the junk.

'Never seen that before,' muttered Mr. Loveless, 'must make a note of it.'

Lunch was Welsh rarebit with a dash of Worcester sauce. There was still an hour before the Queen's Speech via the satellite, he'd look at his notes. His concentration was disturbed by a familiar clang. There was movement in the scrapyard. Nothing alarming, commonplace, especially if anything new was added. He only had himself to blame. Besides the site, indeed the whole island, had a noisy reputation if local mythology was to be believed: a place of fire and fiery apparitions.

The din stopped. The Queen's Speech and order was restored. The final chords of the National Anthem had barely faded when a new sound emerged. A steady throb that moved Mr. Loveless to the window. Gazing in the direction of the scrapyard, a shaft of light was reaching out into the night lengthening with every throb.

'What is it searching for?' he whispered, a tad uneasy. He gave himself a large Scotch and returned to the window. A frightening thought loomed before him.

'You're not searching for anything. Something is searching for you. You're a guiding light, a flight path.' The island was to get a visitor. The decanter was feeling lighter.

The birds began to sing, the blackbird, the blackcap, the robin, filling the night air with their lusty trilled notes, their calls answered by other birds who flocked to the roof top. It's impossible, they're supposed to be asleep. The big scavengers were the last to arrive, the skuas and the stormy petrels taking the prime perch on the balcony, ignoring the human who peered through the window.

Mr. Loveless's fears began to fade, his home was obviously a venue but he wasn't part of the entertainment. He opened two windows of the Advent Calendar he'd neglected. A stormy petrel and a skua, the two birds on the balcony. Hardly festive. The last window remained, the 25th. Strange, Advent ended yesterday. What bird would be released? None, only the statement

"To be arranged."

Something was afoot.

The chatter petered out and the bird song died. A glow began to radiate between the avenue of trees, a great ball of light that transformed into a wondrous creature. An avian beyond the fossil record, a ghost from an uncharted past, a bird for Beltane. Its warm breath ruffled the feathers of the spectators as it hovered above them with all the majesty of an angel. The bird's eyes, multi-faceted and diamond bright, blazed into the night, its rippling plumage shimmering and dazzling. Then one by one its wing feathers began to fall, exploding briefly and dying like spent rockets. As ephemeral as a mayfly, the creature faded and dissolved into the night.

Mr. Loveless, trembling, wiped his eyes.

'How cruel. How cruel.' he blurted. 'Just another three days and my master would have viewed this wonder.'

He slumped into the chair and sobbed. Regaining his composure, he collected his present from under the Christmas tree; a DVD from his master.

A skua appeared on the screen with a stiff familiar walk. It gave a nod and began to speak.

'Merry Christmas Robert. Yes, I'm back. I was on your balcony earlier, the third skua on the right. I gave you a friendly flap but you were a bit overwhelmed. I've had a lovely day. Splendid lunch, my old self was very tasty and you did present it so beautifully. Pity I had to share it, but you mustn't be a gannet. Wasn't the show spectacular? Our bird outshone any stuffed turkey. I'm quite an impresario these days and it was all at short notice.

You must look me up in the New Year. If you get two splashes on your left shoulder give me a wave. Must fly.'

The screen went blank.

Diana Ashman

Christmas mind dump.

Christmas wishes to one and all,
But, look out,
the writings on the wall.
Charlottes mind dump, I recall.
Now is the time to sort it out,
Remember,
Make a list, make a chart,
Of why, and when, you need to start.
Prioritise, that's the key,
Can be difficult, you'll see.
Put your aims and goals in place.
Keep them handy, just in case.
Now, take a breath, have a beer.
I wish you all a happy new year.

A little verse to say thank you.
From, Diane

Free Flight

Shake rattle, rock and roll
I take a walk on the wild side,
Nearly every day.
I swallow the drugs,
To take it away.
Sometimes, they make it worse.
What a curse.
I trip most days,
Not in a purple haze.
But over the mats and the rugs.
My eyes are pinned, no It's just wind.
My coffee spills out of my mug.
I have a tremor in my right arm.
People, think it's caused by the gin.
So what with my shuffle.and all the kerfuffle
That comes on with a drop of a pin.
You can guarantee, if I try to explain,
My words will be mumbled and muffled.
Next time you meet. Someone like me
Shaking, staring, rocking or reeling,
The symptoms you see might be of Pee Dee
I'm not drunk on drugs, or high as the ceiling.
Am just me, quite able.and still breathing.

Night shift.

The full moon, it's intriguing shadows and shapes, if you stare long enough you can convince yourself there must be more to that vast endless expanse they call the universe.

A cry of, Mum your going to be late it's nearly half past eight broke my chain of thought, it's ok, I don't start till nine fifteen tonight, still looking at this lunar wonder, I pulled myself up from the comfy old chair.

Thinking I really must get my bottom into gear. Rushed into the hall, grabbing my bag as I went, shouted see you later as I shut the front door. Gravel crunching underfoot as I walked across to my very old little red mini, known as the mighty min. It looked good in the moonlight,

Putting the wooden close peg on the choke, only way the thing will stay out. I pulled out into the country lane, the moon still bright, shining across the fields, thinking it's really good living so close to where I work, In the distance the hospital lit up looking like a fairy castle. I had been working there on the acute psychiatric ward for nearly six years, in its day it had been called a lunatic asylum, Ah, full moon, still looking towards the hospital, could be an interesting night.

I pulled into the car park, to be greeted by our new junior doctor who looked about twelve,

Love the car, he grinned, bit of a classic now, yes, I said like me, he looked puzzled

Works well, needs TLC, and a few new parts, now and again, well best get a move on. My bleeper hasn't stopped all day, full moon, I said, as I slammed the door. That went straight over his head, I thought. And hurried into the ward, the noise hit me, like a smack in the face. Tamla Motown, greatest hits, could only be.......... A voice boomed out, Di, it's a party, have just called Buck house to ask if they need a DJ, gonna call back in the morning, Hello Brian, I said trying to be professional, you should put some clothes on when you call the queen, he raised his eyebrows, really, but she can't see me, no I grinned but I can. See you in a minute, I dashed into the office. By now I five minutes late. I stopped dead in my tracks, sitting in the corner was a larger than life clown, and next to him a wizard, complete with wand. The rest of the team just burst out laughing, come on in, welcome to happy hour, the staff nurse said with a hint of seriousness. I sat listening, I just knew tonight would be interesting, it's that full moon.

The handover, can be a bit long winded, but tonight it was essential to have all the appropriate information, due to the fact there had been three new admissions one section three of the mental health act.
The larger than life clown began to speak, I realized that it was Jim, who was a member of staff, Nev, I laughed, fantastic outfit,who's your sidekick, the wizard, spoke, I have not had time to change, he moaned, so much paperwork to do, with that, the place exploded, with, welcome to the real world, Should have used your wand, I muttered sarcastically, the wizard, also known as
Gladys, gave me the evil eye look, I was used to his ongoing whining, Jim did a sort of, under the breath, moving on, rolling his eyes.
Yes, Brian , we came across him this afternoon. We had just started our charity fun day in the village, when a car braked so hard its back end. Spun round, the driver's door flew open, and out jumps this chap, wearing nothing but a pair of Ray bans and a floppy hat, both having the price tags on dangling in the breeze. He took his hat of, waving it above his head as he shouted in a very loud deep texas droll, I'm a DJ, I play night or day, he had no idea who we were, but I thought to myself, oh dear Brian your not well.
All this happened so quick, I didn't have to call the police, they arrived just as Brian began dancing to that pineapple song, apparently, he had left a trail of destruction, after helping himself to

the hat and sunglasses in Boots, then kissing the girl on the till, saying, just of to rob a bank, then legged it.

We decided to escort him to the police station, as we knew Brian. He was brought to the ward on a section 2, that was later changed to a 3, because he was seen to be a risk to himself and the public.

Having put two of the upstairs windows out, to the tune of Love the sound of breaking glass.

Both Wizard and clown now feeling quite exhausted, what had started off as being a fun afternoon, had turned into somewhat of a chaotic nightmare.

As they left the office, you could hear Brian, singing Face of a clown, along with, a chorus of choice swear words.

The handover continued, just the two other new admissions, as the rest of the clients were known the night team.

I sighed, glanced out the large office window, there it was suspended in the ink black night sky silent peaceful, the full moon. How could something so beautiful cause so much disruption down here, Bizarre I thought …. but true.

Handover done and dusted, the day staff went home, I walked out onto the ward, It was surprisingly quiet, no music, and a small gathering of people stood laughing around one of the arm chairs, I walked over, and there sat the DJ, zonked of energy, fast asleep snoring with his mouth in the fly catcher position, legs akimbo. I'll go fetch him a blanket.

I smiled, as I walked of to the linen cupboard, thinking, perhaps tonight just might be calmer than I expected.

Hold that thought, as I looked up the ward, no music, just Brian singing " aga do do do , push pineapple", and trying his best to get everyone to join in.

Otto Dix.

My mind only sees the illusion of life, disjointed,
Merciless I take my brush, outline the ugliness onto my bland canvas.
Severe, extreme, it grows until an explosion of hate, love and lies extracted,
From the depths of where, who knows,
I empty the dread,
It seeps into the picture, now complete.

Prager Strasse 1927

Twilight trees.

Branches a black lace of silhouettes'
Against a yellow hue, as the sun sets.
The twilight trees, waiting. Dark and silent
Their bare lifeless bark eager for that moment,
When the warmth of spring, will flow.
Then buds appear, unfurl and grow.
The twilight trees, now wave their leaves,
On that gentle warm evening breeze.

Jenny Fisher

Grouping

I looked at Sophie waiting for an answer. At three years old I knew she was beyond my understanding and control. A year ago she was constantly rearranging the clutter on the floor into groups. The groups would depend on colour, size or shape according to her mood at the time. She was particularly concerned about Jamie's clothes when he threw them around. More disturbing was the ability I had noticed lately of being able to see into peoples' minds. It was almost psychic. She seemed able to assess their characters and personalities. She is now ten and that ability has grown. I am at my wits end and don't where to turn.

That day I had suggested going to the beach. As I waited for her answer I thought, this is ridiculous, she is only three and I feel she is on top, *she* is alpha.

'That would be nice', she said. 'Let's go then.' I breathed a sigh of relief. I desperately wanted this break. It had been a split second decision. Hard work and the breakup of yet another relationship in addition to the stress over Sophie's behaviour had taken their toll. It was hot and the sky was a dazzling blue colour with only a few wispy clouds in the sky. When I told him my six year old son, Jamie jumped up and down with excitement.

'Mummy, can we take our buckets and spades? Jamie was squealing with excitement.

I was planning to go to a beach about 20 miles away. It was fairly secluded with good sand, but more important to me it also had rocks with some interesting pebbles on the beach. I am a keen geologist and wanted to introduce Jamie in particular to the art of collecting and classifying into groups. I knew this would suit Sophie as well.

'Come on Jamie, help me get things together. Buckets and spades of course. Water and sandwiches, dodgy jam biscuits, sun cream, hats and swim gear'. I was thinking aloud, trying to get my head round this. Then I thought of course, we will need a couple of beach blankets to sit on and some collecting bags.

At last we were ready. I strapped Sophie into her car seat and Jamie sat next to her in the back. I leapt into the driver's seat and we were off. Jamie didn't stop talking for the whole journey. In about 45 minutes we were there and we parked in the allotted area next to the beach. I saw a few parked cars but not too many. *Good*, I thought, *I don't want too many people around.* I hated crowded beaches.

Time to unload. I was not prepared for the sheer weight of it all. I knew I would have to hold Sophie's hand to guide her over the rocks and even though I had a ruck sack full of drinks, sandwiches and sun cream on my back it was practically impossible. I was nothing if not obstinate and started walking. Jamie went ahead with his bucket and spade.

'Can I help, Miss'. I heard a voice at my elbow. I turned and I saw the voice belonged to a man. He seemed to be by himself. I looked at him closely. He was slightly built with dark wavy hair and stubble on his chin. He seemed OK.

"Thank you,' I said and gladly let him carry the blankets and chair I had brought. I felt Sophie judder and shake slightly. I looked at her and saw she had turned pale. She returned my look and shook her head. *What on earth is going on with her?* I thought. I ignored her and followed my rescuer down to the beach. I felt really grateful and was not going to be rude to someone who had offered their help. My children must learn to appreciate kindness in others.

I looked around as we walked and I thought *this is paradise*. I counted four family units sitting in the sandy area. There were about 3 young children of Jamie's age and 2 of Sophie's age. There were also three teenagers, two boys and one girl. No arguing at the moment. I also looked closely at the pebble area. *Good, lots of different types*. Good for grouping lessons.

Most of the families were sitting close to the sea, I looked for a space nearer the rocks but still on the sand. At last I found an ideal spot.

'Thanks so much,' I showed my appreciation to my helper by touching his arm lightly. I saw Sophie scowl and turn away. My helper smirked his acknowledgement and walked off.

Jamie wasted no time. He pulled off his outer clothes and started digging. 'Wait.' I called and pulled out the sun cream with which I covered his skin. The next hour was idyllic and there were no distractions apart from eating our sandwiches which Sophie managed to get covered in sand. I must admit I regretted the absence of an ice cream van.

When we had eaten I took the children to the pebbled area. I asked them each to pick up 16 pebbles and look at them closely. Sophie was particularly fascinated as I knew she would be, and even though she was only three she quickly understood what I wanted them to do. Before Jamie had spotted similarities and differences she had sorted four groups. The two basic groups she chose were round smooth ones and irregular ones. The irregular ones were mainly flint of course but the other ones she divided into stones which had black inclusions and those without. I was astounded, she was only three.

We took the pebbles back to where we were sitting and I sat down to rest and reflect. The children happily played and my eyelids gradually drooped. It was hot and so relaxing. I watched the ripples on the sea and listened to the soporific sounds they made as they lapped the shore. The teenagers were eating their lunches and fiddling with their mobiles. I was unable and unwilling to stop myself from drifting into sleep.

I heard shouting. *Why was that?* I was on the beach and it had been peaceful. My eyes opened and I peered around. *Where were my children?* I panicked and jumped to my feet. Then I saw them.

They were both near a family group who were seated about 10 m away. Jamie was trying to pull Sophie away and back to me. She was resisting and pointing her finger at one of the teenagers who I had seen earlier. I could see two shocked parents, one young child and another teenager.

''You bad', I heard her say and she turned to the father and pointing at him she said, 'you good.' I rushed across and lifted her into my arms.

'What are you doing?' I asked her. She looked at me with her huge blue eyes and answered me. 'I am grouping, like the stones.'

'I am so sorry,' I turned to the parents. 'I don't know how to apologise enough.' The mother looked at me strangely. 'You have a weird child there, I'm glad she's yours and not mine.'

Time to go home. I gathered up everything from the beach and stuffed as much as possible into the rucksack.

'Mummy, we haven't been in the sea. I want to swim in the sea.' 'No Jamie, another time.' As I was rushing to the car, Sophie looked at me again with her innocent eyes and asked,

'Mummy, what did I do wrong?'

All the King' Horses

Humpty Dumpty approaching the wall 1460-83

It was 1460 and the small dark haired boy shrieked in anger. "Mother, George is pulling my hair again and calling me names. Tell him to stop." He was eight and was constantly bullied by his older brother George.

"Hush Richard, I'm sure George didn't mean to be nasty." Cecily Neville only wanted peace. She was the Duchess of York, the granddaughter of John of Gaunt who was the third son of Edward 3rd. Her husband was the Duke of York, the great grandson of Edward 3rd. When the War of the Roses started in 1455 he was the leading contender for the throne. She had only just heard the news that her husband, brother and her adored 17 year old son had all been killed in the latest skirmish with the Lancastrians at Wakefield. She was numb with grief.

"You and George must be friends. You're going on the boat tomorrow to Utrecht and I don't want any quarrels."

As she went out of the room George, three years older, pulled a face at Richard and whispered in his ear, "You are a humped squirt and I don't like little brothers who tell tales. You wait, I'll get you."

Richard Plantagenet crept to a corner of the room and slumped down with his head in his hands. He was a highly strung and sensitive child who suffered from ill health. He had a curvature of the spine which gave him a lot of pain. At the moment he desperately wanted his eighteen year old brother Edward, who he worshipped. Edward was charismatic, good looking and popular with everyone. Now Edward was under the patronage of the Earl of Warwick who was supporting him in his bid for the throne.

Richard and George spent the next year in Utrecht in the Low Countries. He hated it. Then came the welcome news.

Richard looked up in amazement when his brother rushed in to tell him. George never told him anything but this news was very exciting. "Guess what's happened. Edwards won a great victory and we're going home." He couldn't wait for the next day, he was so excited. It did finally come and his heart jumped with joy when he saw the coastline of England come into view.

At last I will see Edward again. But I wonder where I'll stay now.

He soon knew, he was to go to Middleham Castle near Durham which had been in the Neville family's possession since 1270. There he was to undergo his knighthood training until he was sixteen. His uncle the Earl of Warwick had organised everything. While he was there he regularly saw his cousin Anne who was Warwick's daughter and they became inseparable. Isobel her older sister also came and there she met George who she would later marry. Edward visited his brothers often and when he did it was the high light of Richard's week.

In 1470 came the shocking and distressing news that Warwick had betrothed his daughter Anne to Henry 6th son Edward of Westminster and soon they were married. Richard was distraught. He had been planning in his own mind to marry her himself. However the marriage only lasted a year as Edward died in 1471. Richard didn't wait long and he and Anne were married in 1472.

How things changed quickly in Richard's tumultuous life. The previous year in 1471 Edward became King Edward 4th when the old Henry 6th died. Richard was delighted and remained hugely supportive to his brother. Edward was very popular but he was definitely a womaniser and had many mistresses. In 1474 came the Big Bombshell. Edward secretly married Elizabeth Woodville. Five years older than him and with two children from a previous marriage to Sir John Groby. What was worse was that he had been a Lancastrian.

"This is terrible news." Richard expressed his concerns to his friend Sir John Howard. "She is a commoner and she comes with a clan of awful relatives, all lusting for power. Not only that but he was engaged to the daughter of Louis 11th of France. This marriage isn't really legal." But his motto was 'Loyalty binds me' and he remained fiercely loyal to Edward. This included siding with Edward against his brother George, now the Duke of Clarence who continued to rebel against his older brother. George was supported now by Warwick who had changed sides. Eventually George was executed for treason later in 1474.

It seemed a happy marriage and Edward remained besotted. Edward and Elizabeth produced 10 children some of whom died young. Two younger brothers, Edward who briefly became Edward 5th and Richard.

Humpty Dumpty sat on a wall – 1483-85

Another upset, Edward the indestructible died unexpectedly in 1483. His heir was the boy Edward who was 12. Richard was appointed Lord Protector as advocated by Edward in his will. But of course he came into constant conflict with the all-powerful Woodvilles for power.

Now he was plagued by a growing suspicion that Edward 4th's father was not the Duke of York, Richard was only his half-brother. Edward was born in Rouen and the Duke was fighting elsewhere at the time. Thus the boys had no right to the throne.

"*What do I do?* The suspicion was gnawing at his insides. Richard was now married to Anne Neville his cousin and they had one child, a boy who was very frail. In July 1483 Richard made the decision and declared the two boys illegitimate and he himself was declared King by the Royal Council.

Previous to this he had been based in the North. He was very well regarded and completely fair in his dealings. Of course he was all powerful as king but he had to fight to keep his power. He had many enemies amongst the numerous Lancastrian supporters. The War of the Roses which had started in 1455 was still on-going. These supporters included Margaret de Beaufort who was continuing her obsession to put her son Henry Tudor on the throne. His claim was so weak and questionable it wasn't considered by Richard to be valid for one moment

After a great deal of heart ache Richard declared the two boys illegitimate. They were in the Tower awaiting the older boy Edwards's coronation. They were never seen again.

Richard searched his soul. "Where are those boys? They are only children. Somebody must know. I only wanted them to be prisoner for a while and I could have had them transported to Europe. I'll be blamed for this, I know I will."

He was right, he was blamed and this blame was exaggerated by the Tudors and he was turned into the extreme villain that he was not.

However the council had declared him King and he was crowned in July 1483. His two years in power were marked by his fairness in government and by great personal sadness. His son Edward died in 1484. He and his wife Anne were devastated. Anne in particular never recovered and in March 1485 she died. Richard likewise never recovered from this second cruel blow.

Now he had to face Bosworth. Henry Tudor had managed to collect together an army of 5000 mainly French mercenaries to march across England.

Richard of Gloucester sighed as he looked down on the battle field at Bosworth in Leicestershire. It was a hot day in August and he really could have done without this. All the human loss which would inevitably happen tomorrow. All because of this Welsh upstart Henry Tudor. Of course it was really due to his insufferable mother Margaret Beaufort who had from birth wanted the English throne for her son. He sighed again and considered the armies. There should really be no trouble tomorrow. He had 8000 men and Henry 5000, no trouble at all. He knew of old though how random the scales of fortune could be. He had no trust in Lord Stanley for a start, he was the husband of Margaret Beaufort.

Humpty Dumpty had a great fall 1485

The next day came as it always does. Richard was ready. Once again he surveyed the bleak field in Leicestershire. He was satisfied but he did notice that Stanley had positioned himself in a neutral place. *Why? It wasn't what they had agreed.*

Richard had amassed his army into three sub-groups. His friend from his teen age years Sir John Howard, Duke of Norfolk was in command of the vanguard, The Earl of Northumberland had the command of the second group and Lord Stanley had the third.

With ear splitting cries the vanguard attacked.

Now is the moment. Richard watched for the second group to attack as well. There was no movement. *Why?* He watched and waited, still no movement. *Treachery!*

This is the moment for action. It has to be done. He shouted for support and led a cavalry charge into the centre of the enemy's ranks where he knew Henry Tudor was placed. It was a foolhardy and brave action and it almost succeeded. It didn't because of Lord Stanley's treachery. He had positioned himself where he could see which way the battle was going. Now he saw Richard's vulnerability and he charged in to surround Richard and hack him to death.

All the Kings Horses and all the Kings Men
Couldn't put Humpty together again.

Richard saw Stanley's men and knew it was all over. They swiped at his horse and dismounted him. He still fought bravely and he kept on fighting. But he was surrounded and they hacked at his helmet and then his skull. They hacked at his legs and his back and he was dead. It took death to stop him fighting. They stripped him naked and took him to Leicester to be dumped unceremoniously in a grave in a monastery. His body was discovered over 500 years later in a car park. He has now been given a burial befitting a King and he now lies in Leicester Cathedral.

He was the last King of England to die in battle and his death ended the Wars of the Roses. He was the last Plantagenet King. He was on the throne for two years only yet he is the most reviled monarch in our history.

I put the case that he was essentially a fair man who throughout his life fought pain and ill health. He wanted to do right by his country and he remained true to his motto, 'Loyalty binds me'. He was the victim of his time. The time of switching loyalties in the name of Power. The acquisition of Power by Fair means or Foul.

I rest my case.

Game of Mirrors

I screamed and ran from the room. My mirror game wasn't real. It shouldn't be played this way, leaving me dead and lying in a pool of blood with a knife in my back. Terrified I ran from room to room searching for a way out, but I was getting more lost with every second. There were so many rooms, all filled with mirrors.

In my early teens I had discovered the mirror game that offered alternative choices in other realities. This time it had been initiated by violence. During a heated argument I had thrown a small mirror at my husband. One shard had cut my hand as it shattered on the floor. No choices here in this house of mirrors.

A door lead me into a magnificent but crumbling hallway. Cobwebs trailed across the elevated ceiling and engraved archways. There was a persistent and overwhelming smell of decay and rotting wood. Doors lead from the archways into other rooms. I opened one door and inside saw to my horror, three decomposing bodies in defensive positions. Slamming the door I ran. Anywhere to escape that smell of decomposition. Frantically I pushed at a heavy highly decorated door. It opened at last. The room was massive and packed with mirrors of every shape and size. Cobwebs and dust covered them. No reflections could be seen. *How do I get back?* My mirror had been broken. Now I panicked and ran frantically from room to room, seeing my dead body in my burning desire to escape.

It was then I heard a muffled, disembodied voice which seemed to echo through the walls.

'Find two identical mirrors and you will find a way.'

This I must do and I will find them. I started to search.

Summer Holiday

I looked round trying hard not to be noticed. There was a vast expanse of rippling sand on both sides of where I was sitting. The sea glinted in the occasional bursts of sunshine. My mother had dumped me in front of a half open hut amongst a large group of children. I looked at the hut more closely. There was a stage at the top with red striped curtains at the sides. I was near the front and felt hemmed in. For some reason some of the kids were yelling out and after a while I realised what they were shouting.

"Come on Punch. We want Punch." I was confused and felt very alone. All the others seemed to be with brothers and sisters. I wished my mother hadn't left me by myself.

"Now then Tom," she had said. "This will be the highlight of your holiday. I'm not going to tell you about it but there will be lots of children and you will make friends. I want you to stay there until I collect you. You might have to wait a bit but I will come, so wait. Here, I'll give some money for an ice cream."

She practically threw a couple of paper notes at me and left me on the beach. I watched her as she left. I saw her throw her arms round a man who looked even to my inexperienced eyes, much younger than her. I didn't like him.

Then I was alone. Seven years old and left to watch a Punch and Judy show. I felt miserable and bereft. The boy next to me suddenly kicked me on the shin. I yelled out with pain and he laughed,

"All by yourself then? Nobody to look after you then?" He would have kicked me again but the show started. The curtains were drawn back and Punch appeared.

He had a club in his hand which he announced was a truncheon and he wacked it down on the shelf again and again shouting loudly,

"That's the way to do it; that's the way to do it"". He scared me. Then Judy appeared with the baby in her arms. She asked

Punch to look after the baby. Punch 'looked after' the baby and ended up battering him. Judy appeared and then she and Punch quarrelled very noisily and Punch ended up battering Judy. It reminded me of the fights mum was always having with her boyfriends. It was all very scary and confusing, In fact I was terrified. However a few ideas were planted into my head that day.

Punch ended up killing someone and the hangman came to hang him but he cleverly avoided that and the hangman ended up being hanged himself! I thought it was clever that he changed his name from Punchinella to Punch. *What a clever idea to do something wrong and then change your name.* In fact he was clever all the time. I was so impressed when the crocodile stole his sausages and then he got them back.

The show lasted an hour and I was scared but mesmerised at the same time. The other children stood up and their parents collected them. I looked for mum but couldn't see her anywhere. I was used to this and wasn't worried.

I'll look for an ice cream stall and spend that money mum gave me. I saw a stall not too far away and started walking towards it.

"Hello laddie, all by yourself then. You can save your cash, I'll buy your ice cream. Your lucky day – eh?" I looked up and saw a tall man with ginger hair and a spotty face. I remember thinking, *OK, so you don't like him. It would be nice to have an ice cream treat though.*

He bought me the ice cream cone with a choc and flakes. He suggested then that he could take me home in his car. He had some sweets in his car. He took my arm and pulled me in the other direction. I was beginning to feel scared.

"Hey, you. What do you think you are doing? Leave my lad alone"'. It was my mum screaming at the nasty man. She ran over and yanked me away. The man turned and ran off. She chased him for a bit and then gave up.

Her boyfriend joined us and looked angrily at me as if it was my fault. "You should have stayed on the beach like she said".

"Bbbb – ut" I started to protest but mum pulled me to her.

"Come on, let's find the car and go home.'" The air in the car was thick with anger and unspoken accusations. We reached home and mum and I stumbled into the hall. The boyfriend started lashing into mum knocking her on the floor. It was just like Punch and Judy.

All I could think was that I had to stop this man who I had decided I didn't like at all. I ran into the sitting room and grabbed an iron poker in the grate. I was Punch. I rushed into the hall where mum was lying on the floor, blood gushing from a cut on her leg He didn't see me. I raised the poker into the air and hit him on the leg. He yelled in pain and fury and collapsed onto the floor near mum. My anger wasn't yet dissipated and I raised the poker again, this time aiming at his head.

"No Tom", mum saw and shouted at me but it was too late. The poker landed on the side of his head and he slumped face down and unconscious. I raised the poker again and again. Each time I shouted out, "that's the way to do it, that's the way to do I'".

I killed him that day. I felt no remorse. I didn't like him, you see. Mum was hysterical but when she had calmed down I took charge. I had a plan, for that day and for the rest of my life.

Witches Brew

I followed her as she hurried along the lane. She was muttering under her breath but I couldn't hear the words. She was wearing a long dress made of thin delicate material that I had noticed before. It was red with black imprints. As I looked she shivered violently and hugged herself. I increased my speed so I could get closer. I wanted to hear what she was saying.

'Witches, brew, must get, know they are near'. I heard some words but they were garbled and didn't make sense. She was running now, along the lane towards some woods which lay ahead.

I had noticed her that evening in the pub. I was consoling myself with a pint and was with two friends. I had finished my half term exams and knew I hadn't done well. She was by herself sitting in the corner by the open fire. As well as noticing her thin clothes I saw how skeletal she looked. Her face was pale. There was no make-up and she had long straight hair which grew almost to her waist. She was twisting her hands together continually and hardly touching her glass which looked as if it contained ale. One of my friends noticed her as well. He nudged me,

"What's up with her then? She looks a strange one. Go on Pete, give it a go. I bet 5 quid you won't get anywhere with her. "I did feel a strong compulsion to approach her and stood up. Walking across I felt fascinated and became aware of a sort of force surrounding her. I can only describe it as a type of magnetism that emanated from her. She was slightly older than me but what does that matter? As I approached I felt the temperature change. Even though she was next to the fire I felt a cold draught. She didn't seem to notice my approach and stared straight ahead.

"Hiya, you a stranger here then? Can I buy you a drink? You look as though you need another one."

She did change the direction of her gaze but seemed to look right through me instead of at me. There was no response to me or my words. She continued to look in my direction but there was no change of expression – yet. But suddenly her face did change into an ugly grimace and she stood up. She lurched towards the door and went out into the fog outside. What did strike me as very odd was that she had no coat and it was cold out there. So much for my attempt at friendship. I went back to my jeering and mocking friends.

But I had lost my desire to celebrate in spite of continual back slapping and reminders that 'after all, it is Hallowe'en, lots of strange people around', I felt bound to follow her.

I stepped outside. The pub was on the corner of two lanes and there was open country and woodland nearby. It was foggy and I could just make out her figure in the distance. She was making her way down one lane towards a gate which led to a field. I ran to get nearer. I wanted to follow her but I didn't want her to know she was being followed.

Then I heard her words. I struggled to hear them and all I could understand was the continual reference to witches. In spite of myself I shivered. *What was going on?*

I could tell she was terrified of something and was freaking out.

She ran into the woods, I followed. She ignored the path and negotiated the thick growth of trees. It seemed to me that she knew where she was going. For myself I had not been into these woods before and soon I was utterly lost. I had to keep her in sight. She had reached a clearance in the trees and was surrounded by a ring of ancient oaks. She slowed to a stop. Frantically she twisted her head in every direction, violently flailing her arms around at the same time. She was obviously looking for something or someone. I noticed that she was now barefoot, somewhere she had kicked her shoes off. I heard a voice.

"Maggie, my dear. What are you doing here? Where have you been all these years?" A strange figure had appeared out of the trees. She was the classic old crone, with a pointed hat and black cape. She had long straggly hair and a long sharp nose. She looked back at the trees and called,

"Come Rosie, see who has joined us this year. " A second person had emerged from the woods. She was wearing a pointed hat as well but appeared to be slightly younger. She too had long dark hair and again her nose was long and, yes, witch looking.

Maggie rushed over to them and fell at their feet. "What did I do? I'm so glad to see you. Where am I? It all seems so strange. Even these woods are different. Tell me Ester what did I do? I was with you and Rosie. You were preparing a brew for the acolytes to drink." She was shaking and could hardly speak.

Esme took off her cloak and wrapped it round Maggie. "My dear girl, you know what you did. You submitted to the sin of curiosity. You weren't even experienced enough to be an acolyte but you showed promise." Maggie had stopped shaking and her face showed a mixture of understanding and guilt.

"I'm sorry I drank some of the brew. That was stupid. I wasn't ready. This place is dreadful, people don't dress properly. Its indecent sometimes, girls show their legs and they talk in a funny way. I want to go home."

"You've travelled in time dear. You are now in the future by about 200 years. Going home is possible but risky. We can try but you must understand the dangers."

I trod on a twig and it cracked. I had been watching and listening, not willing to believe this was really happening. Maggie reacted immediately. Suddenly she was there, facing me.

"And who are you pretty boy? We can't allow this, watching witches in the woods on Hallowe'en is not permissible."

"That's the man in the strange inn who tried to buy me a drink. He was nice to me, he must have followed when I left. Don't use your powers on him. He's harmless." Maggie seemed to accept that but then.

""We can't let him go back and tell everyone what's happened. That would be against all the rules. People must never know that we really exist. I know what, we'll give him a mild dose of some lovely medicine I have to block his memory. It might come back later but they will never believe him.'

What else could I do? I had to go along with it. She took a bottle out of the hidden recesses of her inner garments and told me to take two swigs. I did so and felt most peculiar. An odd swirling sensation gripped me and I couldn't think what I was doing in this woodland. But I did notice this lovely girl in the wonderful red dress. I didn't even see the old hags. I didn't know that they had instructed the girl to hold hands with them to form a ring and they had started chanting. I rushed towards the girl and held her hand and inadvertently joined the magic ring.

Everything went grey after that. I was vaguely conscious of far off voices, some shouting in consternation.

I looked round. My God where was I? I was aware of engines working and an enclosed space where I was resting. Someone was leaning over me and trying to waken me. I glanced over and saw a girl resting next to me asleep. The girl was familiar, she was wearing a red dress.

"Come on mate, wake up. We're nearly there. We've almost arrived, the Red Planet is waiting for us. Time for your duties to start.

The truth dawned, I was on a space rocket, destination Mars. I leapt up and stepped across to the nearest porthole. Yes, the Red Planet loomed large and clear. I glanced down to where Maggie was still sleeping.

Lynne Stone

Beautiful Lady

The lift doors opened and Bonita and Paolo swept into the hotel foyer, showing their membership cards they were ushered into the private members area. They took their regular seats overlooking the pool.

Bonita flicked back her chestnut hair and sat back crossing her long tanned legs, flashing her toned thighs, while tapping her perfectly manicured hands nervously on the glass table in front of her.

"Relax darling you look perfect."

"I am worried, I am just not sure you've picked the right pair this time Paolo."

"Trust me I have never been wrong yet."

"There is always a first time." she replied quietly.

He patted her diamond adorned hand reassuringly and signalled to the waiter "Two very dry Martinis please."

Bonita looked at Paolo and said "Here they are let's get on with it. As she spoke a loud brash American voice shouted, "Gee Beautiful Lady thanks for waiting for us."

Marnie waddled over to the couple and leant forward to kiss Bonita who instinctively pulled back not wanting cheap American lipstick on her perfectly made up face. Art flopped down beside his wife and mopping his sweating brow he said "How do you guys stay so cool in this heat"

"Simple we are Brazilian this is normal for us." He clicked his fingers and called the waiter over "Drinks for my friends please."

They sat back and were chatting when Paolo's phone rang. He stood up and said "Alo"

He turned to the table and said I need to take this call and with that he went outside onto the deck while Bonita looked anxiously on.

A few minutes later he was back and speaking in their native language he snapped at a worried looking Bonita, with that his phone rang again and once again he excused himself.

By now Bonita was becoming agitated and she kept looking anxiously through the glass door at Paolo who was pacing up and down the balcony gesticulating wildly all the while.

"Forgive me Beautiful Lady but is there anything wrong? You look worried."

Bonita winced at Marnie's choice of name for her and answered quietly "No no its just business we chose a bad time to come away Paolo will sort it out."

She sat back in her seat and tried to steer the conversation away from her husband.

It was at least half an hour later before he came back into the lounge, he looked pale under his Brazilian tan.

"I am sorry you will have to excuse me from dinner I have problems that need to be sorted quickly, do you mind looking after Bonita?" he directed his question to Art and Marnie. To Bonita he whispered, just loud enough for the American couple to hear he said "Darling things are not looking good, I will be back as soon as I can." She patted his hand reassuringly and said "its fine I am sure Marnie and Art will look after me."

With that he walked out leaving an uncomfortable silence behind him.

Bonita eventually broke it by saying "This is unforgiveable of us we are spoiling your evening, I can eat in our suite if you would prefer?"

"Rubbish dear we know only too well what it's like to run a multi- million dollar business, problems never leave you even on holiday."

Bonita sighed and taking a sip of her almost forgotten Martini said, "We came away thinking everything was in place, but it seems our most important backer has pulled out leaving us in an embarrassing position financially."

Art spoke without looking at Marnie and said "If there is anything we can do to help Bonita let me know, we are always looking for new investments."

Bonita laughed and said "I am afraid you will need a spare million dollars to get us out of this mess."

Marnie gasped but before she could speak Art puffed out his chest and said "I can do that it's just spare change to a man like me."

Bonita looked over at Marnie who looked as if she was about to faint, and said quietly "Thank you Art it is a lot of money but I am sure you need to talk to Paolo not me."

After a strained dinner where Marnie found it hard to speak and drank too much wine and ate very little Paolo came to find them and Art immediately took him to one side and discussed the finer details. Paolo agreed to draw up a rough contract agreeing to pay the money back within 12 months at 10% interest. Art almost bit his hand off to sign it and agreed to go into town when the ship docked in Gibraltar the next morning as they had some shopping to do anyway and the money would be transferred by lunchtime.

They shook hands on the deal and went off to bed with only Marnie looking less than happy about the deal.

The next day all went to plan and Art treated Marnie to a new pair of diamond ear- rings and a champagne fuelled lunch to pacify her once he had transferred the money over. So they were both in high spirits when they got back to the ship and spent the afternoon dozing on their balcony in the sunshine.

Up in the lounge bar Paolo had left a message with the concierge for them saying they had ben late getting back and would see them at dinner. The Americans sat feeling very pleased with themselves, perhaps for different reasons and watched as the ship pulled out of Gibraltar.

At dinner the two other places remained ominously empty and Marnie said

"So where are beautiful lady and our new business partner Art?"

"Don't worry pet they will be here,"

When they didn't turn up Art made an excuse and leaving Marnie eating her third dessert he tried to call suite 1001 no reply hoping he had the number wrong with heart beating he went to guest services and asked them for the correct room number for Mr and Mrs Suarez.

The receptionist told him to wait a moment while she checked she came back to him and said "Sorry sir we do not have any passengers on board of that name."

Art felt his knees begin to tremble and said "Ridiculous we have had dinner with them every night for ten days the sad they were in suite 1001."

"I will check for you sir."

She clicked away on her computer and said "No sir that suite was occupied by Mr and Mrs Smith and they disembarked this morning in a taxi going to the airport."

Art muttered thank you and stood still for a moment wondering how on earth he was going to tell Marnie they had just lost a million dollars??

Sold my Soul for 20p

Downsizing and de-cluttering was not as easy or cathartic as everyone predicted. Had it been done properly without emotion, my garage would not have been full of boxes labelled Just in Case.

Two years down the line and the boxes remained untouched, the weather forecast was sunshine all the way. I figured it was time to say good bye once and for all. A boot sale that would sort it.

So with a borrowed paste table and high hopes I set off at 6.30am on Saturday morning.

The queue was enormous, I estimated there was around 400 cars and vans as I waited I anticipated the fortune I was about to make.

I soon had the stall set up, but despite doing a trial run the previous day, my stall did not look nearly as tempting in the sunshine as it did in my dismal garage. The problem with doing a sale on your own is that need to leave the stall to go to the toilet. Why is it that despite going before leaving the house and not drinking anything, the need to go rears its ugly head before I even get out of the car?

I wait with bated breath, first few punters are looking for vinyl records and jewellery, I sit down pour a very small coffee, even at 8am it is already hot. Did I bring sun tan cream? No of course not.

My first customer, actually that is a polite description, he looked more like a tramp. I shuddered he picked up a bottle and stood stroking it, he had the worst comb over ever and I had to look away when he opened his mouth, it wasn't the single yellow tooth, but the fetid breath he breathed over me and my table. I didn't speak, but he did he proceeded to tell me that he had just bought a fishing reel for £5 from a right idiot on a stall further down the aisle. What a bargain he said the stall holder had wanted £10 for 3 reels but he beat him down for one. What an idiot, I stifled a giggle and he put the bottle back and swaggered off, convinced he had a real bargain. I quickly wiped the bottle thoroughly with a disinfectant wipe and put it back on the table.

There was a steady flow of people, clutching their 20p's that seemed to be the only coin available. I was reminded of a conversation I heard on the radio with Alan Carr, he did a boot sale and was asking £15 for a toaster and it was another stallholder who politely pointed out that when customers said they didn't want to break into a twenty they meant 20p not a note.

I had high hopes for my next customer, she was smarter than most and spoke perfect English. She picked up a pair of my evening shoes and examined them closely, there wasn't a mark on them. Probably because the only time I wore them, I caught my heel in the hem of my dress and landed sprawled out on the dance floor. My damaged knee was a constant reminder of my age. Now I didn't think £2 was too much for these diamante trimmed satin sandals, but despite the fact they were actually too big for her she bought them and knocked me down to £1.50. It was as she went to walk away that she turned to tell me that she was going to a posh ball and it was in Dubai. She was talking down to me and walked away when I merely said I had been in Dubai earlier in the year and I hoped she enjoyed it. She just snorted and I am not ashamed to admit I said as she walked away, that I hoped she fell over in my wrong size £1.50 sandals.

By this time feeling downhearted I had a customer who wanted my Bose Speakers for £10 only trouble was they were the wrong colour and he had forgotten to go to the cash point would I give him my bank details and he would put the money in my account. What do you think I said? Granted I know it can be done by phone but at a boot sale, really?

I did manage to get a toilet break, husband turned up knowing I would be desperate. I was only gone ten minutes and when I got back he had increased my takings by 50p. He said he had sold a pair of earrings to a very snotty woman .As she paid for these earrings she said condescendingly to my husband, "You won't be able to make money like this when we come out of the EU. Luckily my husband was the other side of the table and he restrained himself. Simply retorted that he didn't discuss politics with strangers. Anyone who knows him will be impressed at his control.

I managed to get rid of a few of the bigger items and started to pack up as in the last half an hour I hadn't taken a penny. Just as I was about to close the boot a woman came along and picked up a sarong which I wanted a pound for, she offered me 5p and finally agreed on 20p. I slammed the boot and drove away had I really sold my soul for 20p?

The Night Before Christmas

Jacob looked around his front room. He hadn't bothered with Christmas this year, in fact he hadn't bothered with anything since IT happened. He picked up the solitary wrapped present and fingered the label. It would have to go out with the rubbish now, he wasn't allowed to speak to his little friend over the road any more. It was a shame he would have loved the train set. One of his neighbours and he hadn't quite worked out who it was yet had branded him a pervert. A pervert for goodness sake, he had been too upset to defend himself just shut his front door and cried. Eighty years old and he couldn't even remember the last time he had shed a tear, maybe when his beautiful wife Eleanor had died. But nothing like this. This accusation had turned his life upside down. "Cat come and talk to me." he called to his pet who nonchalantly strolled over to him and jumped up on to his lap.

"Do you think I did anything wrong Cat?" he asked.

Cat purred and curled up on Jacobs lap loving being stroked. "I felt sorry for the lad he was sat on the doorstep crying, I mean where was his mother, eight years old and locked out of the house in the rain. What else could I do? I just asked him in for milk and biscuits. Seems his mum works late every Wednesday and he is supposed to wait on the doorstep until she gets home. That's not right but anyway we got on well. You saw that didn't you Cat? He liked you too. Not as much as he liked the trains. Forty years it took me to build that railway in the summer house. Forty years and now I don't even have the heart to go down there."

Cat stretched and meowed loudly, "Sorry Cat I forgot to go shopping it has been so upsetting, fancy some nosey old bag reporting me for abducting a child. It was the first time that young Danny and I forgot the time we were having so much fun playing with the trains. He was only half an hour late, late enough for someone to tell his parents he was in my shed with me. I mean shed? It's a summerhouse for goodness sake."

"Can you wait for dark and I will go to the corner shop and get you some cat food I promise."

Cat jumped off of Jacobs lap and slunk out of the room and Jacob sighed as he heard the cat-flap slam. Now he really was alone. Christmas was always a difficult time since Eleanor had died. Jacob thought he had coped really well for the last ten years, first Cat had strolled in one day and made his home with him, Jacob loved the ginger tom, it was pure laziness that stopped him thinking of a name after all he answered to Cat so that was good enough. Then came Danny, a train enthusiast so rare in the younger generation, they had become mates until the evil neighbour intervened. He walked into his kitchen and as he passed through the hallway he saw yet another white envelope one the mat, he picked it up and put it with the pile on the hall table. Hate mail he was sure. He put the kettle on and looked in his fridge. Christmas Eve and the fridge was empty. He checked the freezer, nothing, then the cupboards, nothing. It didn't matter to him, but to Cat that wasn't fair it wasn't his fault. Jacob straightened up and looked outside, it was almost dark, with a bit of luck he could get to the corner shop without being seen.

Just as he was putting on his scarf, the doorbell rang, he froze Oh please not the police, should he open the door or slink away into the kitchen? No he was a man all be it an old one so he opened the door.

"Mr Grant?"

"Yes who are you?"

"I am Danny's mum can I please come in. I have been putting notes through your door but you don't respond."

Jacob ran his fingers through his thinning grey hair and said distractedly "Look I haven't done anything wrong this is all so unfair."

"I know, I am sorry this is all my fault, Danny has only just told me how good you were to him." she started to cry and went on. "Danny's dad ran off and left me a year ago and I have really struggled. I have to work and I don't have any family to support me I shouldn't have listened to Mrs Cameron."

"So that's who it was, some people have nothing better to do."

She looked uncomfortable and then said "Yes it was."

"But Danny is too young to be sitting on the doorstep waiting for you to get home, I looked forward to him popping in after school."

"I know that, I just wish I had known, but he never said."

Jacob twisted his scarf and said "I was on my way out."

"I wanted to ask you to come to Christmas lunch, Danny would love that and I promise I will put it right with the neighbours."

"I don't even know your name. I'm Sally please for both of us."

Jacob thought for a moment he thought of his empty fridge and another day with only Cat for company and said, "Thank you I will come but only for Danny."

"Thank you, it will make his Christmas" with that Sally left leaving Jacob wondering what on earth he had let himself in for.

Whatever he was going to eat tomorrow didn't change the fact that he had to go out and get food for Cat. Mission accomplished the corner shop was empty, cat food bought and he bought a few essentials and as he was leaving he spotted a bottle of fizzy wine, the kind his Eleanor had been fond of. Well Sally had made an effort, so would he.

Christmas morning he was up early, showered and shaved he fed Cat and picking up the solitary present and bottle he walked across the road to Sally's house.

As he walked up the path, the door flew open and Danny ran out shouting "Grandad!!"

Jacob looked flustered Sally laughed nervously, "Mr Grant is not your Grandad."

"But I've never had a Grandad Jamie's got two."

Jacob handed over the parcel and smiling said "Happy Christmas and I am not Mr Grant it's Jacob," he ruffled Danny's hair and said with a catch in his throat "I've never been called grandad before, you can on one condition you let me help you set up your present ."

Danny gave a whoop and began ripping the paper of the train set.

The Walking Stick

The day started off much as any other for me. I wouldn't call it normal because normal as I see it should be getting out of bed looking forward to the day ahead, having a leisurely breakfast and leaving the house smartly dressed for a well-paid job. No normal for me is, the feeling of dread that overcomes me the minute I open my eyes, rarely do I have breakfast, the fridge is usually empty, gone are the days when my fridge was well stocked. My wardrobe consists of clothes from my hippy days that's all I own.

Today was marginally better in so much as the sun is shining and I have days' work. I don't have money for the bus so I take my trusty bicycle Maud from the shed and begin to cycle to my modelling assignment. That is an over glamorous description, what I actually do is sit naked in a draughty old barn. While eccentric, even older than me, would be artists, sketch my overweight sagging body.

I took my usual route, all the time pondering how on earth I was going to pay my rent this month. At least I was getting paid for this day's employment but jobs were getting scarcer by the day. Although it was still early the sun was hotter than I had expected. I stopped my bike to catch my breath, it was then I remembered, my bottle of water, still all alone in my fridge, I of course have no money with me to pay for more so my only hope is to plough on and hope I will get at least a cup of coffee when I get there.

I get back on my bike and head towards the barn, then I see it laying across the road a carved walking stick, its silver handle glinting in the sun. I have two choices either ignore it or pick it up. I choose the latter, if I left it a car would surely run over it. I am going to be late so I tuck it precariously under my arm and pedal furiously through the village.

No time for coffee, the class are waiting for me, I strip off and sit on the cushions and try to focus my mind on anything but the fact that I am here a fifty something (I can't even admit to myself my real age) woman naked on a grubby cushion in a smelly old barn. Instead I am in the arms of a famous rock star on his yacht in the Bahamas, once that could have been possible but now just a dream. My mind wanders, oh god I want to pee I should have gone before I got here, but I was late, then I remember why I was late, the walking stick. I have seen it before but right now I can't remember where. I can't see the clock but my body is desperate to move, fortunately I am handed a threadbare towelling robe and I make a dash for the port-aloo before anyone else can get there.

Still pondering over the walking stick and curious to look closer at it I went round to the back of the barn where I had left it propped up against Maud. It had been polished and well looked after, if only I could remember where I had seen it before. Come to that what on earth was it doing in the middle of the road? No time to think about it now I am being called back to finish my session.

Clutching the few pounds I am paid for the morning I make my way home only stopping to buy some essential food in the corner shop. While I am there I ask Mrs Riley if she recognises the walking stick, she does and points me in the direction of the old Manor House at the end of the village as I live at the opposite end I go home and have a sandwich and a coffee before setting out to return the stick to its owner.

The house looks neglected and the garden once beautiful now overgrown with weeds and brambles, I knock on the door and an elderly man who I instantly recognise as Eddie Brown, he used to run the Dog and Duck on the village green. He spots the stick and tears spring to his rheumy eyes, Oh come in he says where on earth did you find it? Before I can answer Eddie has limped through into the kitchen, he puts the kettle on and I explain that I picked it up on the main road. He wrings his hands and says "It was my grandfather's and passed down through the family to me, I use it daily, but unfortunately last night I caught some lads trying to break in and I ran after them or tried to. I threatened them with this but one of the lads grabbed it and ran off."

"It was lucky I found it then, much longer and it would surely have been crushed by a car." I said and stood up saying I had to go.

"Before you go dear, I did report this to the police and there is a reward for returning this."

"A reward?" I questioned.

"Yes it is extremely valuable to me, I am so grateful to get it back." He goes over to a biscuit tin on the shelf and hands me a bundle of notes. I hesitate but only for a moment and say, "Thank you I am glad to help and then I add if there is anything else I can do?"

Eddie sighed and said "I don't suppose you know anyone who wants a housekeepers job do you? My last lady had to go and look after her sick mother and won't be back."

I looked at his lost face and around me at the mess in the kitchen and taking a deep breath I replied "As it happens I do know someone. When can I start?"

Wild Thing

It may have been the sink full of dirty dishes or the grey skies outside that made me feel blue that Tuesday morning. I felt old, neglected and unloved, but then surely I was just like most middle aged women whose family had fled the nest, and yes I do mean fled my two sons had gone off to find themselves a few years ago and sadly never came back.

I forced myself to get on with the mundane chores, wishing I was anywhere but here in my kitchen with not even a packet of biscuits to tempt me, the radio playing softly in the background. Then it happened while I was staring at last night's gravy stained dishes, I heard it "Wild thing you make my heart sing"

The years slipped away, I began to dance around the kitchen singing along with the Troggs. I knew every word, when it finished I sat down and let the memories wash over me. Neville "the mod Blake" his name was, so good looking the only boy I ever met that owned a full length leather coat, which he never took off. I was the envy of all the other girls on the estate, I swear he was the love of my life. Wild Thing he used to sing to me, I was flattered, looking back I realise he was only trying to get into my knickers, did he? I am not telling!

We used to walk down by the canal most nights during the holidays, sit watching the barges go by, making plans, which we never got to fulfil. Life took over we had both failed at school so we had to get jobs, no college for us.

The beginning of the end came when Neville took me to a party, this was my one and only introduction to drugs. Harmless he told me, purple hearts admittedly they did look like those mauve sweets that grannies used to eat, Parma violets I think they were called. So as not to look out of place I took a couple. The rest of the evening passed in what I now call a Purple Haze, it ended with my parents being called out to collect me from the police station. Not my finest hour but I wasn't charged just cautioned but of course my parents were furious and forbade me to ever see Neville again. I took no notice and we still met most days but the inevitable happened, we slowly drifted apart and I began to go out with more sophisticated (or so I thought) boys. Lads that drove cars didn't turn up in leather coats riding a clapped out bicycle. Neville went away, and I never heard anything more from.

To this day hearing that record playing still sends shivers down my spine, I am sixteen again and so in love.

On days like this I confess I searched Friends Reunited, Facebook and googled his name, nothing he did not appear to exist. Was he a figment of my imagination? Surely he is out there somewhere? I am not unhappy with my life, just lacks excitement.

Exciting is how I remember my relationship with Neville. So on grey day like this I find myself back on the internet, searching for a trace of him. Then I found it Linkdn he was working at a large company in the next town. Nothing else about him the rest was left to my imagination, which I admit I let run riot.

The offices for this company were impressive and years ago I had tried to get a job with them but I never got past the first interview, it didn't stop me being extremely envious of any one who did work there. I never achieved the high salaries that they paid. Neville however had managed it, I wondered if he lived in one of the new houses in the new village that had sprung up opposite the canal where we used to walk. Perhaps he even had a swimming pool, why I sucked my bulging stomach in at this point I don't really know.

The telephone rang interrupting my reverie, my friend inviting me for coffee. I hastily pulled myself together and drove off to meet Sally in the new coffee bar. It was the first time I had been there so I was relieved to see her sitting in the window waiting. We chatted for a while and as I stared out of the window I realised it was the very company I had been thinking about earlier, so off I went again perhaps Neville would walk down those steps and come sweeping in here spot me and …. Sally interrupted my thoughts

"For goodness sake where are you today, I'm talking and you're not listening?"

I mumbled a reply and shortly after made my excuses and went to do some shopping as I walked slowly past the building a chauffeur driven car pulled up and I stopped to see who was going to get in or out of it. My heart was thumping wildly, the doorman came swiftly down the steps and opened the door, to my disappointment out stepped a very glamorous woman, I stopped fumbling in my bag and turned to leave only to come face to face with the doorman. Neville, my Neville old, grey and very forlorn looking. I couldn't speak for a moment, but he looked straight through me and walked back up the steps. All my dreams shattered in that moment I walked back to my car quite forgetting the shopping I had set out to buy. Once in the car I took a deep breath and switched on the radio "Sunny well yesterday my life was filled with rain "Sunny You smile at me and really ease the pain Oh the dark days are done." Sang Georgie Fame, I smiled to myself now that reminded me of Tommy!

Margaret Jennings

It's a Mystery

My name is Paul and everyday I live between the trouble with geraniums and Aunty Flo.

Every day, I get up and stack myself together, one cube atop another, until I have formed a brand new and idealised version of me. One that can liaise between the geraniums and Aunty Flo.

Some days I end up with my nose out of kilter. Some days I have two ears on one side and none on the other. But, you know, people very rarely notice. I try to notice other people.

I was in the corner shop the other day, waiting for my ham to be sliced. I like watching the ham being sliced. A woman had been eyeing me up. My mother aways said that I should expect that being so handsome and all. But I would have preferred to be able to watch the slices of ham lay themselves one on top of the other. It is so elegant and predictable, and in its own way, beautiful.

That woman annoyed me even more when she said, 'ahem' and gave me a coy smile.

"You have food on your face,' I said and moved my hand to indicate the side she should wipe. But there is a universal truth, a mystery if you like, that no matter which side you indicate, people will always wipe the other side.

'No, the other side,' I said.

'Oh, that's a mole,' she said.

It was not a mole. It was egg if I am not much mistaken. Raw, smeared, egg yolk - and here she was thinking I might find her attractive.

'You need to wash it off,' I said, 'it is not a mole.'

She touched her face again. On the correct side this time. She took a hanky from her bag and dabbed at the spot when I nodded to indicate that she had hit the mark.

I had totally missed the ham being sliced. It was already in the brown paper bag and being handed over. The cash register rang and I sorted through a handful of coins to find the right pennies.

'Do you think I should use make up to cover the mole?' she asked, ' do you think that would make me more attractive?'

'No,' I said, 'nothing will make you more attractive if you insist on wearing your breakfast on your face.'

I left the shop. I was looking forward to a ham sandwich with lashings of piccalilli. And I had the very serious business of Aunty Flo and the geraniums to deal with. I could spare no brain power to solve the mystery of why people always touch the wrong side of their face when you tell them there is food there.

Perhaps when I arrange my cuboid self another day, there will be space for the calculation of the scientific probability. It should be fifty fifty surely. And yet it never is.

Ventri Thingy

Sarah thought nothing of popping the tablet in warm water then gulping the water down in three swift swallows. It was her preferred method of taking tablets. Most other people said it was best to balance it on the back of your tongue before taking a swig of water. Someone else said they always demanded medicine, and yet another said they never took medication of any kind.

Sarah always took her tablet before she went to bed. It was not a sleeping tablet. She took it then because it was built into her routine. Teeth, face cream, tablet, bed, quick read of book, then light out and sleep. Deep dreamless sleep.

But this night, this particular night, when nothing was especially different and she had followed her routine with saint like virtue, she was troubled with dreams where her tummy talked to her. And boy was it full of opinions.

Next day she googled talking stomachs on the internet. Universally it seemed to say that she had eaten something she oughtn't before going to bed. Or that she was keeping some deep, dark secret repressed.

She knew that neither were the case. Her life was an open book. Her heart was an open heart and she lived for the betterment of the lot of mankind - donating to charities, helping old people in their homes for no charge, babysitting when people needed her to.

Today she was off to see Joan. Two tone Joan as Sarah called her, who was either happy or sad, never anything in between. Today Sarah was happy to find Joan in a very happy state of mind. Sarah was busying herself with plumping up cushions and wiping down already wiped down surfaces, when to her surprise her stomach said, 'Joan , you should turf this woman out, She's stolen all your china and that necklace you thought you'd lost.'

Joan looked up, looked around, the smile on her face froze a bit, 'are you one of those ventri thingies then Sarah, you know, with the puppets?'

Joan was looking directly at Sarah's face and saw not a whisper of movement when words emptied form her stomach again.

'And she knows where your husband is. You know, the one that ran away. Not the one you killed off.'

Both Joan and Sarah looked stunned.

'That's not you talking is it, Sarah,' said Joan.

'No,' replied Sarah.

'It sounds a bit parroty to me. Have you swallowed a parrot?'

'Don't think so.'

'Then how did you get a parrot in your stomach and how does it know all this stuff?"

'I…' said Sarah.

'I knew about the stuff you took,' said Joan,' and I never cared a jot about it.'

'I never knew about your husband,' said Sarah.

'No,' said Joan, ' and I bet we both have a few more secrets we don't want getting out.

They talked about the problem and a possible solution for many days. Which is why, seven days later, they fished a parrot out of the toilet and swiftly pulled its neck.

Mick Cooper

Food glorious food

The family left the Palladium afternoon performance still singing one of the songs. 'Food glorious food cold jelly and custard.'

Having sat through 2 hours of the musical 'Oliver' they were still unsure of the words.

The early evening traffic was building up to the usual London rush hour congestion.

As they happily walked along the street, Dad said "OK, so where are we going to eat?"

There were no instant suggestions as they strolled occasional gazing into shop windows at things they could never afford. They passed several fast food shops but none of the family was that keen on any of them, so they moved on.

Further on down the street they came to a darkened shop front.

The sign above the window read ' The Coven, A restaurant of the unknown. Find us on the Witch Report.'

They were uncertain at first. "Come on, let's try this one, it looks a bit weird, but I'm game for it!" said Dad.

Still in doubt they all looked at each other for someone to make the first move. "Oh Come on, I'm hungry," said Dad as he led the way in and slowly they all followed him in.

They saw that the room was empty of other people. It was painted black and looked very drab. Mother noticed several cobwebs and shivered at the thought that there might be spiders.

There was a log fire in the grate roaring away and a cauldron boiled on it. On the mantle above it was a row of china frogs and toads lined up. Some of the furniture looked very old.

They all sat at the nearest table to the door unsure about their surroundings. The kids started giggling as they spied a stuffed black cat in one corner. Mother turned to her husband and said "I don't like this place, it's giving me the creeps."

He tried to calm her saying, "Oh don't be silly, it's all for show, It's meant to spook you. I'm really scared" he said as he smiled at her.

He reassured her by saying it's probably one of those new types of themed restaurants and added "It all looks very good. Someone must have spent some time making at look this spooky!"

"And they did a very good job too!" she added firmly. Dad looked around but still there was no staff making an appearance. He yelled "Waiter!"

A dull dressed elderly woman seemed to appear from nowhere. The children started giggling again when they saw her long nose, beady eyes and missing teeth.

Quickly the kids stopped giggling, and took fright as she glared at them. Her eyes glistened and they felt very uncomfortable and wriggled in their seats.

Dad asked "Could we have a menu, please?"

The strains and lyrics of the Oliver songs were now long forgotten, but they could hear some very strange music.

The woman handed then each a menu, said nothing and then disappeared as instantly as she had appeared. They were in disbelief as they read;-

"Fried bats wigs, Toasted fox, Fricasseed Hedge hog, and boiled squirrel."

Dad suddenly felt a chill slide down his back and he looked sheepishly towards his wife.

There was silence and one by one they looked up to each other.

For a change the kids were as silent as the room now was.

Call ESP if you like, but somehow they all knew what to do next.

They quickly rose, and as silently as they could opened the door and tip toed out of the building,

Taking a large gulp of fresh air as they escaped they laughed and giggled at what might have been a close shave with who know what. Hurrying down the street and rushed straight into McDonalds

Heroes

The battle was over, the horrors of Hougoumont had ended.

It was a battle like no other battle before it, but the battle was won, and we, were the heroes. There were bodies everywhere.

We buried our dead and tended our wounded, taking time to recover our sensibilities.

Later we took many hours to walk across the land that was Belgium and were pleased to reach the coast.

The channel was not kind to us. I never saw greener faces throwing their insides overboard.

The good feeling of Portsea Island English soil under our weary feet brought quick relief to our shattered souls and bellies.

We walked on North over the hill of Portsdown and down along a leafy lane and came to an inn on a crossroads.

Some of us wanted to press on but most of us could smell meat roasting and the relishing thought of washing some down with a mug or more of ale was not possible to resist.

The landlord and his wife made us very welcome and his pretty daughter, a comely wench who flirted with the men, was a sight for sore eyes.

We told them our tales as we fed and drunk well.

Bye and bye the landlord returned with a board, and words scrawled upon it, with charcoal.

He said, the nation would be ever grateful to us all and nailed the board to the wall. Then he said in our honour he would name the inn, 'The Heroes of Waterloo.' Some of us could read those words on the board.

After resting, we said our goodbyes with the thought of our homes in minds.

Many of our men set off heading for Surrey and London. Others went to the West. We all took the road that began the rest of our lives.

Holy Smoke

The Reverend Andrew Saunders walked through the ancient lych-gate and along the path towards the church door. He could see Tom Spencer pushing his trusty mower as he manoeuvred between the grave stones.

Tom stopped and yelled, "Mornin' Vicar!"

"Ah yes! good morning Tom, another lovely day thanks be to God," he tried replying over the mower noise.

"Have you settled into your new home yet Vicar?" questioned Tom.

"Oh yes, just about sorted, thanks!"

Tom eagerly added, "You're gonna have full house on Sunday Vicar.

All the villagers will want to see the new man. Just to see if you're meek as a lamb looking for a flock or a man breathing fire and hell and damnation, beggin' yer pardon Vicar."

Andrew chuckled to himself as Tom bowed his head and touched his forelock, by way of an apology for his words.

"Tom?" said the Vicar.

Tom looked up and then turned the mower off hoping the vicar wasn't about to give him a sermon.

"Yes Vicar?" he answered as they came face to face.

"Tom, er, there's a large box, a large wooden chest like box in the cupboard under the tower stairs. It's locked, have you any idea where the key is?"

"Oh no Vicar you don't want to bother with that, noooo I shouldn't touch that if Ize were you!"

Tom hurriedly turned away before the Vicar could ask anymore and restarted his mower.

Andrew stroked his chin uncertain about Tom's words and then shouted "But why is that!" Tom turned, left the motor running and walked back to the Vicar "Well, yer see,…the old rev, a,…

Reverend Toby, he said it was to be left there and never to be touched by anyone, man, woman, child or beast!."

Again he turned quickly and returned to his noisy mower.

"Oh! Ok Tom, thanks." Andrew walked on towards the church door, still unsure, and even more confused.

He did his usual checks around the church making sure everything was in order, and without any unwanted overnight guests.

Andrew noticed that the ladies had done a fine job with the flowers and a floral aroma filled the church. He settled in the vestry planning to write something for the Sunday service.

His mind was wandering and he found it difficult to start.

Despite the warning, and being very curious, he pulled the chest out from the under stairs cupboard, and stared at it.

"Hmmm ? So why should it not be touched" he said aloud.

The dark wooden box had stained brass plating on each corner, he wiped off some cobwebs and said,

"Well, it looks harmless enough to me, why is there such a mystery?"

He noticed that the keyhole escutcheon was a silver colour and appeared to be glowing slightly in the dim vestry light.

He took a key ring from his pocket and tried several of his own keys but none seemed to fit. Finally a key did slip in but, would not turn. The escutcheon began to glow brighter and he heard a loud click.

"What was that?" He said, surprised to think that it might have unlocked itself, and disbelieving that it actually had."

He tried slowly lifting the lid, and to his surprise, it opened. As he did a whoosh of stale burnt air escaped and hit him full in the face.

"Oh" he shivered, "What was that?"

The box contained rolls of browned paper flaking with age at the edges.

He lifted the top one out and as he did a wisp of something smoke like rose out and circled around him. He watched as it moved and ascended the stairs that led to the bell tower rope room.

Andrew blinked his eyes several times, "Did that really happen, did I really see that?" he wondered. His hair had been blown around and he pushed a lock back from his eyes.

He unrolled the first paper. The writing on it was hard to read, faded in many places and mostly in Latin. Some of the old English words were clearer and he read the date "21st July 16- Sixteen something" he said as he tried to make out the almost obliterated year. Then a name Emma Wilson, and three more barely readable words, 'at the stake'

Gradually the story became clearer. There was also a bound book with the word Burials in gold inscribed on the front cover. He saw that most of the entries were regular burials but none later than the sixteen hundreds. Then he noticed that written up side down,.. inside the back cover, were five names, one of which was Emma Wilson.

"Ah, so maybe these would have buried in unconsecrated ground," he surmised, "Is that why they are written upside down? But where would that be?" he pondered.

Then he remembered that the road out of the village lead to rocky piece of land that was wildly overgrown and known to all the villagers as Aldwich Hill.

It wasn't difficult for him the figure out that it was probably a name that was corrupted over the years and perhaps it was originally and better known as old witch hill. It all seemed a little clearer.

"Perhaps that's where the remains were buried?" he guessed.

The wisp of smoke reappeared and moved slowly around the vestry and eventually stopped by him. To this day he swears that he then heard a voice say 'Thank you' but as clergymen don't usually swear, you may not want to believe him.

The smoke moved away and out of the vestry door into the church and then out into the open air.

For sometime Andrew was speechless, trying to rationalise and make sense of what had happened. Had it happened? Yes it had he was sure. Andrew took a deep breath, and felt contented and somehow fulfilled. He read the remaining paper rolls then placed them all back into the chest and gently closed the lid. "There must be a key somewhere, but where?" he thought.

He pushed the chest back as far as he could into the cupboard under the tower stairs. As he did, he heard a click and for a moment the escutcheon glowed and then faded to black.

He decided to go into the church, sit for a while, and try to collect his thoughts.

After more than an hour and few prayers he left the church. Tom had finished his mowing and gone. Andrew looked up at the blue sky, and felt the warmth of the sunny day. The smell of new mown grass was all around him. The snowdrops were fading but daffodils were in full bloom along the church wall.

"What a beautiful day!" he said aloud and then he returned to the vicarage for his lunch.

Jeremiah's Mystery

Most people believe that the British film industry started in the dim distant past at Shoreham in Sussex but sadly that didn't last very long. Today, we all know Hollywood in the USA is the Mecca for the money makers of the film world. Annual Oscar ceremonies bring to us smiling stars that most of us have never heard of before or since. However, my local newspaper ran a story that shook the international world of film.

Jeremiah Johnson died age 103 and lived most of his life in a sleepy little village near Portsmouth. It was believed that he never moved far from there and died a lonely man in a care home.

Only one of his distant descendants could be found and she lived in Australia.

Arrangements had to be made and his great great niece Alison travelled to England to sort out his estate.

Jeremiah did own his house but it had to be sold when he needed help and to be moved into the home 14 years before.

A young couple bought the house and decided to empty it completely and redesign it in their own modern style. In the process they found a number of wooden boxes in a deep corner of the attic. When each was opened they were surprised to find many small round metal cases, a stack of diaries tied with ribbon and a number of dusty scrapbooks, each with the logo on the front reading Lovedean International Films.

Alison realised that Jeremiah was the owner, director and producer of his own local film making company. The whole collection informed her that for over the years 1913 and 1914 Lovedean was the world centre for what we now know as 'The Movies'.

There were bundles of letters and many fading photographs. The entire contents were removed from the attic and Alison spent many hours reading every item to unfold Jeremiah's story.

She started by sorting through the photographs. Many were anonymous, but some had writing on the back giving names. With a little figuring out, she was able to pick out Jeremiah from most of them. Other names were mentioned but were unknown to her but one name, Molly was more prominent.

The earlier diaries had little detail. 1909 and 1910 were almost empty,

1911 mentioned that he had several jobs during these years but lost them all.

It seems he flitted from one to the next without any real idea of where he was heading. In the 1912 diary there were many mentions of flying and various attempts by British pilots to get airborne, and failing.

"I must try this flying game one day" he wrote on March 27th.

On April 15th she read several lines about his first flight, and successful landing.

Later the same year he joined the Royal Flying Corps. The entry for August 8th reads, "Damnation! I did it again, thankfully I walked away unscathed, but today I bent another Sopwith. Curses on that squadron leader, he's not perfect, anyone can make mistakes. I have had enough."

Jeremiah returned to Lovedean, but whilst in the RFC had found an interest in photography and had purchased a camera. Somehow his interest in a stills camera didn't last. November 21st entry read "Getting good results from the film camera. I have managed to capture many local people on film and local scenery. Might have a go at making a story film, but need a story and some actors.

She waded through to the end of the year but nothing more until the early days of 1914. "Have completed the second of our films, 'The Master's Voice'. Good actors from the local drama society and a charming story should make it more saleable. Have had talks with several local kinemas and they are keen to buy more of my films on lease. First film 'She was his woman' was well received by many full houses. I have met up again with Jock McKay from my RFC days and he is now head of my sales team"

Another page read, "Light not good today, need an all weather studio, could move to a beach like they have at Shoreham, but don't really want to move from here."

Alison turned to the scrapbooks and read many newspaper reports and reviews about Jeremiah's successes. It all looked as though he had finally found his vocation. On returning to the 1914 diary, she saw "Losing young actors who are volunteering for the army. A war approached should I join up?'

She looked at the labels on each of the 10 film cans, and noted the two she had already read about plus 'When day is done', 'Love conquers all' and also 'Jeremiah's mystery'. This title made her wonder, had he actually acted in one of his own films? She was curious about the contents in the can but remembered hearing somewhere that those old films burst into flames when exposed to the air, so she thought better of it.

Reading on through the diaries, it seems that film making became more difficult as only females were available as actors and the story ideas dried up. He began to lose interest and again considered joining the film makers in Sussex but discounted it. One name appeared a number times in that year and that was Molly Hayward, it seems he might have had a soft spot for her, thought Alison.

One of the photographs was a wedding group of ten people and on the back was written ten names. Molly was on his arm and wearing a wedding dress.

Alison was sure he was planning a move to join the Sussex film makers, until she saw the last entry.

"Two options, join up go to war and take a chance of getting killed, or move to the new world, America, the land of opportunity, Film making in style with D W Grittith and if Chaplin and Stan Laurel can make it there, surely I can."

So she wondered did he actually go to America? Did he make his fortune there?

I suppose we would know more about him if he did. She packed away all of Jeremiah's collection and decided to contact the Hampshire Film Archive at Winchester and leave the film cans with them. The written mementoes and photographs were deposited at the local records office. Her short spell of time here in England was running out and she needed to book a return flight to Australia. Alison however, decided to check the passenger lists of ships sailing to the USA. In the library, and after some time, she found what she wanted. Mr & Mrs J. Johnson were booked on the United States Mail Steamer

"New York" from Southampton calling at Liverpool and then to Ellis Island on January 4th 1915.

A further search showed his name in a New York directory a year later but nothing after that. So what happened to them in those in between years? Did they return to England, as they must have done at some time later, or did they travel on to California and have success in Los Angeles and Hollywood?

Maybe we'll never know.

Ted's Naked Conundrum

He slowly opened his eyes and was soon fully awake and ready to greet the new day.

Ted pulled back the bed covers and heaved his bulk out of bed and into the bathroom. After a splash all over with cold water, he walked straight out onto his veranda, stretched his arms out and then, stark naked held them aloft as though reaching for the sun.

A couple were walking by and he yelled, "Good morning," and they smiled back in agreement.

Ted was the owner, manager and chairman of the Sunnyside Naturist Camp on a very secluded 3 acre site, miles from anywhere.

The residents and occasional members always had a busy time with all manner of social events in the club house,... that's when they weren't sunning themselves.

At a recent committee meeting, a social night was arranged and a band booked to provide the musical entertainment on the Saturday evening. The day had arrived and Ted eagerly looked forward to the festivities. Later that same evening as he made ready, he rubbed some aftershave around his chin, and sprayed antiperspirant on other parts, which took a while.

Ruth White knocked on his door. She looked flustered.

"What's the matter Ruth? He asked.

"It's the band" she said with an out of breath voice, "They're here!"

"Oh! That's good, have you let them into the club?"

"Yes I have but there's a problem, they won't take their clothes off!"

"What? Oh! In that case I'll need to speak to them."

They both made their way to the club house.

"Err,... who's the leader here?" Asked Ted. Someone stepped forward, and he continued,

"Hello, I'm Ted Watson, the manager here, what seems to be the problem? What is your name?"

"My name's Astral Oblivion,"

"What?" quizzed Ted, not quite believing his ears.

"Yea mate, well that's me stage name but you can call me Joe. Now look," said Joe. "We can't take our clothes off cause that's part of our act. For one hour during our show we are Ziggy Stardust and the Spider from Mars, for a David Bowie Tribute"

Ted turned quickly to Ruth, "What did he say?" She explained that Bowie used that name on one of his record albums.

"Oh did he? I see," said Ted, "I remember the Laughing gnome and Space Oddity, but lost interest in him when his music got so weird!"

"We didn't know this was a strip joint gig either, guv'nor," said Joe, "and if you let us keep our clobber on, we promise not to play Moonie River, or Fly me to the moonie." The guitarist overheard and added, "Don't forget "Under the moonie of love!"

Or if it's a cold day, "Blue Moonie!" There was sniggering and the bass player added, "What about "Dancing in the moonie light" Or "Bad moonie rising" and that Van Morrison song, Moonie Dance."

Drummers always have the last word, and he voiced "Don't forget the old songs, "By the light of the silvery moonie," or "It's only a paper moonie," no let's not go there."

Very soon the whole band were laughing at their own jokes and giggling like an asylum of schoolgirls.

Ted was speechless and decided to regain control, by adding firmly.

"No, let me explain, we are sun lovers, sun worshipers, we enjoy being here and free from the restraints of the modern life and that includes clothes, we are naturists, this is not a strip joint of any kind."

"Oh Right! But we're a tribute act, David Bowie tribute act and if we take our clothes off, we ain't a tribute to anyone, are we mate? We all wear glittery costumes and paint our faces, just like Bowie, you know, with the lightning flash on our faces"

"Oh yes, I see what you mean." Ted didn't really understand and was quiet again, thinking.

"Hmmmm, OK lads, you just carry on as normal, well not exactly normal for us but, no, you just carry on as you do, you know" Ted took a deep breath, turned and walked away with his head spinning and Ruth trailing behind him. How was he going to explain this to the club members, and what's more to the committee? Some of the naked lady members were not happy with males wearing clothes looking at them, but there were some others that didn't mind.

As he walked out of the club and back into the sunshine, he stopped suddenly.

"That's it, that's the answer." He said aloud as he instantly saw his worries disappear. Ted rushed to his office to make up a new large poster.

"Now what was it he called them?" Ted struggled to remember the name and made a mental note that next time he goes to the health centre, to get new batteries for his hearing aides. He sat for some time trying to recall the name.

He pinned the new poster over the notice board poster advertising the evening social. It read,

For one night only, it's a tribute night to David Bowie by "Mickey Sawdust and the Spiders in Jars" and everyone is to wear clothes as outrageous as possible but only from 7pm to 12 midnight, and just like Bowie, paint your faces with the lightning strike, in pretty rainbow colours.

He was sure he'd cracked it.

The evening went well. The tills rang, people drank, danced and enjoyed themselves saying it was the most fun they had had for years with their clothes on.

In the early hours Ted slipped his naked weighty torso into bed knowing that it had been a job well done.

Several days later at the next committee meeting, Ruth asked for a vote of thanks. They all stood and gave Ted a round of applause for arranging such a successful night.

He smiled smugly and nodded his thanks to each of them in turn. It then seemed as though he heard another round of applause as they all sat down heavily on the cold plastic seats.

Everyone agreed it was a brilliant night and wanted to know when the next one would be.

"Yes," said Ted, "I had already made some enquiries, I have had a couple of quotes from the agency, and they are offering,.... a punk rock group, called,...."

There were murmurings, uncertain that a punk rock group was what they really wanted. Ted continued, "They are called Phil Bailey and the Vomits, they are a tribute act to"

Before he could finish the loud disapproval from all made him stop and look up.

"No, No!" said one, "I don't think that's a good idea, Vomits, no that doesn't sound right to me, it could all get very messy, especially as we are all only wearing our birthday suits."

"Well, hold on a minute," Ted tried to sooth the situation, "That same group also do a tribute show for Bill Haley, you know, him who had the Comets, They call themselves Will Bailey and the Rockets." There was silence and then one said

"Oh yes,... that sounds better, much better."

"A great idea Ted," said Ruth,

"It wouldn't be too difficult for the ladies to knock up some of those dresses with all the petticoats underneath and maybe even fashion some of those coats like Teddy Boy drape coats, just like the ones the rockers used to wear, but,"

she hesitated, "Most of the men here are quite old and most of them have bald heads, no hair at all. The only way they could have a flat top hairstyle like Elvis Presley and the rest, is to wallop each one on the head with wooden mallet." Everybody laughed, all accept Ted who added, "And I don't suppose any of them would feel it."

"Hey wait a minute, that's not right!" said the bald headed man to his left.

Ted ignored him and continued, "But yes, I have that little item covered too.

My brother-in-law runs a company that sells wigs. He's got all kinds of wigs, funny ones and proper ones too. He said he would do a very good deal to any man that wanted one, with a large discount."

Everyone now seemed happier, the Rock'n'roll night was agreed and plans went ahead. After the meeting Ted went back onto his veranda and lay out on his recliner adding a few more rays to his already well tanned,….. ample frame.

Sheila Brown

Black Tulips

Annie was waiting for Paul when he returned from work on Monday evening with a glass of Chablis.

"Hi love," he said, "how was your day?" as he kissed his wife and accepted the wine.

"On the whole it was good but a strange thing happened. Did you send me flowers?"

"Flowers, no I didn't send you any flowers. Why, what happened?"

"Someone sent me twelve black tulips. There was no note with them so I phoned the florist to ask if she had the name of the person who sent them, but they'd been paid for by cash and so couldn't give me her name."

"Her?" asked Paul.

"Oh yes, the florist said it was a woman but couldn't remember anything else about her.

Paul sipped his wine and Annie said "Don't you think the flower thing is a bit strange?"

"Em, yes I do. What have you done with the flowers?"

"Left them in the school staff room. Didn't want them in the house. Who would send me black flowers anyway? It's left me with a weird feeling all day."

"Anything else peculiar happen?" asked Paul.

"No, that was it. Do you think it's something to worry about?"

"I don't, maybe you have a secret admirer? Should I be worried?"

Annie laughed. "Don't be silly. I'm sure you're right, I mean about not worrying over the flowers. But I can't help feeling there's something odd about it. Let's forget it. Spag bol for dinner ok with you?"

"What could be better?"

It was three days since he'd sent Sarah the text. Black tulips. Did they mean something? Was it possible Sarah had sent them?

These thoughts passed through his mind as Paul stood where he was, he didn't trust his legs to move. Annie was right about something being odd about her receiving them. The more he thought about it the more unease he was beginning to feel.

Having managed to make it to the dining table Paul remained sitting whilst Annie tidied up, giving him a brandy before she went to bed.

Toying with the glass his mind drifted back to the day he and Sarah had visited the little white church in the green field. He'd seen the church many times as he travelled the main line to Waterloo but had never been in. Sarah told him the church was called St. Hubert, built in the 9th century, rebuilt in the 12th and 13th centuries and still had an active, albeit small, congregation.

That night they made love for the first time, the start of what became a serious relationship which ended with a text three days ago that took seconds to send.

Were the black tulips the beginning of payback?

June

"Where are my damn tablets woman?" The whining had started not long after he'd gone upstairs. These attacks were happening more often now, the pills were his life saver.

Sitting at the kitchen table she was aware of Keith's voice becoming more strident each time he asked the question. June got up, grabbed her handbag and coat and was out of the front door before she lost her nerve. Her husband's calling now unheard as she walked down the garden path, round the corner and ran for the bus that was, miraculously, coming along the road. This was a good sign surely?

The twenty minute ride into town passed with June feeling a mixture of euphoria and fear. She wondered if the other passengers would notice anything out of the ordinary, would they know what she was doing and call the police? Getting off in Cross Street she went straight to the first floor in Debenhams, searched and found the red summer dress she'd been coveting for weeks, picked her size and paid for it using Keith's debit card. He would never know. Nor would he ever find out about the matching shoes and bag she got in John Lewis. The decadent glass of Prosecco with the large slice of chocolate fudge cake was on him too.

Usually wine brought thoughts she didn't want but today was her fresh start and so she welcomed them as a sort of cleansing act. A decluttering and getting rid of the old in order to bring in the new.

All her 40 years June was what she answered to but she'd always wondered what her mother would have named her if she hadn't been abandoned hours after giving birth and therefore leaving the choice to the nurses in the maternity ward. June was the month she was born so that what's they came up with. In her silliest moments she'd been grateful it wasn't November.

The years with her adoptive parents Margaret and George were the happiest she'd had but cut short by a car accident which killed them both. Six years of different foster parents followed but she was always sent back for being difficult. At 16 she left the home, met Keith in a pub near her hostel. She knew she didn't love him but he was kind and attentive so she said yes when he proposed.

As a builder he brought in good money when he could get work and she got a part time job in a café near the small flat they rented. For six months she felt secure. The first time he hit her she forgave him, put it down to his drinking too much and not being used to it. A month later the doctor in accident and emergency asked how she'd broken her arm, she smiled and said she'd been stupid and not looked where she'd being going, missed the steps and fell on the pavement. She knew he didn't believe her.

That hospital visit had shaken Keith so then he hit her where it wouldn't show. Years of fear and shame at being a human punch bag was what her marriage had become. Then, one day two years ago in June, Keith had collapsed in the bathroom. Heart attack, he remained in hospital for two weeks and the peace she felt then was indescribable. To be fair, when he came home, the physical violence stopped cause he wasn't up to it but then his voice became his weapon of choice. Nothing she said, did, wore, escaped his vile verbal abuse. And still she stayed, there was nowhere else to go.

But, today, when the whingeing had started and he was in the bedroom and she could see the front door from where she sat, the thought of what might happen to him if she wasn't there became her hope of salvation.

Three hours after leaving the house, she returned, opened the door to complete silence. Her heart skipped a beat as she took the stairs one at a time. Keith was half in, half out of his chair, as if reaching for his tablets on top of the dressing table. They were too far away and death released June from her prison.

Back in the kitchen she had a cup of tea with a chocolate digestive then dialled 999 with a beaming smile beginning to light up her face.

What a load of nonsense

Off to the surgery he goes with his ailment
The doctor is perplexed, he has never seen a big toe so bent
And set in cement
Wherever he walks he leaves a huge dent
Oh well he says I was at an event
Went for a walk and left my beer to ferment
And thought of the mess made by the government
The strikers who face police harassment
The forces that implement
The sentence of judgment
Lucent
Are those in the moment
Of being nascent
Unless it should happen on the pavement
Quotient
That word is resplendent
But carries no sentiment
Or is known for its temperament
Things were becoming urgent
The doctor's impatience he could not vent
As off to A & E his patient went
Why his big toe was bent and set in cement
Will never be kent.

Sue Cornell

All the King's Horses

Three days after my mother disappeared, a man walked into our house and claimed he was my father. I was ten years old. Grandfather was in his chair by the kitchen fire; he struggled to stand; his old legs could not raise him. Grandfather's eyes blazed with anger and his mouth strained to speak, but no words came. Sinking back into the chair, he seemed to grow smaller.

The stranger surveyed the room. He was tall and dark and I recognized my features in the cleft chin and heavy brow. His clothes were shabby apart from polished boots and a smart black coat. At last, his gaze came to rest on me.

"Get me food and liquor, boy."

I looked over at Grandfather, but he was staring fixedly into the flames, tears of rage on his ancient cheeks.

"Now, boy."

Early next morning I watched from my attic window as our visitor made a thorough survey of the farm. He stood for the longest time looking down at the cove where our skerry was beached. The boat had not been used since Grandfather was struck down. The tall figure descended the steps to the beach and disappeared from my view.

I was helping Grandfather to eat his broth when the man came back into the kitchen. He took off his fine coat and hung it on the peg, then helped himself to bread and rum. The ticking clock measured out my fear in long minutes.

"We are going fishing, boy, you and I; quickly now, while the light holds."

Grandfather clutched at my arm with his good hand.

"The boy is coming with me, old man."

An iron grip on my shoulder, I was marched across the yard and pushed down the steep steps onto the sands below. The skerry had been dragged to the tideline and I stumbled towards it across the shingle. Behind me, the man splashed through the breaking waves; he had removed his boots.

"Hurry up!"

I scrambled aboard.

The boat rocked gently. He positioned the oars and began to row with a strong, steady rhythm. The shore receded as we headed out to the open sea. I realized that the boat was empty apart from a sack beside the man's bare feet.

"Where is the fishing gear?"

I peered beneath my seat. Nothing. I looked up to find he was staring at me with eyes as hard as flint. Not a word was spoken.

Beyond the headland the man stopped rowing and calmly pushed the oars away from the boat. I watched in silent horror as they floated out of reach. He drew an axe from the sack, stood, steadied himself and swung the blade with all his might into the wooden hull. After dropping the axe into the sea, the man who said he was my father slid into the water and began to swim towards the shore. He didn't look back.

I was alone in a sinking boat, far from the shore. I could swim but had never ventured so far out before. I clung to the side as water gushed through the jagged gash in the planking. Desperate for help, I scanned the shoreline. A stooped figure was at the top of the steps; Grandfather?

The sinking vessel lurched as a huge wave rose up, higher than I had ever seen before, a wall of water topped with sea foam that heaved with monstrous shapes, surging towards the shore. I was tipped into the boiling sea; gasping, I fought to remain afloat. Cold overwhelmed me and the weight of my clothes dragged me down until the waves closed over my head.

When I opened my eyes I was on the beach, exhausted but alive. Sitting up, I realized that I was surrounded by hoofprints, already filling with water, melting into the sand. The polished boots remained above the tideline, never to be claimed.

Later, wrapped in a blanket, I watched as Grandfather burned the smart black coat on the kitchen fire.

Boundaries

I walk the boundaries of my life
a geography of place and time –
sad circumferences and glorious frontiers,
extremities of mine.

Then:
inhabiting the confines of my mind, I
created worlds of words and images,
calculations and predictions, a perfect
and limitless
fictional sanctuary.
Reality transformed.

Now:
my spirits soar,
tethered to earth by
beloved bonds of my choosing.
Perimeters expand,
possibilities clarify;
our shared horizons
crystalize.

Beyond borders,
shadowy fears
diminish and dissolve
becoming no one,
nothing.
Boundaries shiver and
melt into mist.

Boundless,
I reside between

your heart
and mine.

June

When they were two streets away from the school gates, June stopped, removed her blazer and tie and crammed them into her bag.

"Got any money?"

"I've got my bus fare." Norah was flustered.

"I need two bob, Nor; I'm dying for a fag."

June was several yards in front by now; Nora had to run to catch up.

"How will I get home?"

"Don't worry about that; Des can take you later."

Norah felt a wave of panic engulf her. "But I'll be late. They'll be expecting me."

June swung round and stared back at Norah in disgust. "Oh, for God's sake! Bugger off home to mummy then."

Norah felt tears prick her eyes. She swallowed and took out her purse. "Wait, June…"

June had puffed her way through two cigarettes by the time they reached her house. Overgrown hedges loomed over the small front garden which was home to an upturned beer crate, a battered scooter and a thriving population of nettles. The front door was ajar, beyond it a cluttered hallway.

"Will it be all right?" Norah whispered.

"What..? Of course – why not?"

June slammed the door open with a crash. Norah stumbled over a heap of shoes.

"Junie, is that you?"

Norah followed her friend through a cluttered kitchen and out into the back garden. A woman, hair in rollers and dressed in just her bra and knickers reclined on a towel.

"You're home early; just in time to do me back. Who's this?" The woman lifted her sunglasses and squinted at June who stood hesitant in the doorway.

"This is Norah, Ma. She's new, just started at school."

"Pleased to meet you, Norah."

"Hello, Mrs Marshall."

"Call me Pauline. No need to hover in the doorway. Sit down; make yourself at home." She gestured at a deckchair. "Come on then, Junie; cream me back while the sun's still out."

June reached across for the suntan lotion.

"I can smell fags! Let's have one Junie, I'm dying for a smoke."

Norah sank into the sagging deckchair and immediately wondered how she would ever get up again without floundering like a fool. Why had she agreed to skipping afternoon school? There would be hell to pay at home if they found out.

She'd never had a friend like June, who was now lying next to Pauline, sharing a cigarette. Around her the garden was bursting with life. Runner beans, grasping tendrils heavy with blossom engulfed cane wigwams; raspberry bushes dripped with ripening fruit; dog roses and honeysuckle nodded in the hedge. An enormous striped cat emerged from the undergrowth and proceeded regally up the path. After pausing to gaze at June and Pauline, the creature leapt effortlessly onto Norah's lap.

June laughed. "Jasper knows a good cushion when he sees one!"

"Don't be mean, Junie, Norah's got a lovely figure. Men like a bit of flesh on the bones." Pauline got up. "Time I got dressed. Does your mum like to get a bit of sun, Norah?"

An image of her mother, frowning and buttoned up to the chin, flashed into Norah's mind. "No, Mrs Marshall, not really."

"I'll make us a brew."

Jasper began to purr loudly, flexing his claws. Norah wondered if her uniform would be covered in his hair and how she could explain it at home. She smoothed the soft fur and wished she didn't have to worry.

"What's up?" June was staring at Norah in concern.

"Nothing. What time is it?"

"It's early yet. You looked so worried then; what were you thinking about?"

"I can't be late, June. I should've stayed at school and gone home on the bus."

"Des'll be here soon. He'll take you." June looked guilty. "It's my fault; I shouldn't have made you come with me."

As the sun measured time across the sky, an apple tree cast a long shadow over two girls on the lawn. Wasps browsed the fallen fruit. Dark clouds began to gather.

An hour later, Norah and June were in the back of her stepfather's taxi. Des was singing along with the radio and cracking bad jokes.

"Cheer up lass; how about this one: what's the difference between bogies and Brussels sprouts?"

"Oh, come on Des, you're just not funny!" June complained.

"Children won't eat Brussels sprouts!"

June gave a slow handclap as Norah stared silently at the passing houses.

"Here we are." Des pulled up in a quiet side road. "Your friend sure lives in the smart side of town, Junie."

Norah got out of the car. "Thanks, Mr Marshall."

"I'll come with you. I'll explain." June began to get out.

Norah was already walking away. "No, thanks. It's okay. I'll see you at school."

"Bye Norah." June shouted. She felt a sudden chill.

The other girl waved as she turned the corner.

"Goodbye June."

On the Third Day of Christmas

Late afternoon of the best kind of cold, bright December day. A splendid sunset glowed behind shadowy rooftops and the looming silhouettes of trees. Pear Tree Lane on the edge of town was usually quiet, the busy traffic on the High Street a distant murmur; on this day, however, a loud, steady hammering intruded on the peace of the neighbourhood which was sleepily digesting its day after Boxing Day turkey leftovers, mince pies and selection boxes.

When he was sure the "For Sale" sign was securely in place, the man from GoMove jumped into his van and drove away. He was unaware that his excavations had disturbed the thorny sticks that had once been a floribunda rose bush called "Together Forever", a wedding gift. Martin, watching from the bay window, did not notice the last withered leaves tremble and fall onto the frozen soil.

The sun sank lower behind the bulky blackness of the church and disappeared. As the last rays faded, shadows deepened under the brooding yew trees and a harsher chill gathered in the darkening streets. A sudden icy wind sent dead leaves skittering, rattled fairy lights and ruffled the feathers of pigeons roosting miserably in the naked branches of plane trees.

Full dark now. The wind's freezing fingers did not disturb Rosemarie as she made her way home. A fox, emerging cautiously from a garden onto the opposite pavement, froze as if sensing some unseen danger, then bolted back to safety. Rosemarie, on silent feet, turned into Willow Road - not far now. There was the pillar box on the corner, a familiar landmark. Ahead, a man spoke reassuringly to his dog as it whimpered and tugged on its lead.

Martin was alone in the front room slumped in an armchair. His feet were resting on a coffee table amongst empty cans and a half-eaten slice of Christmas cake. He struggled upright to add another log to the fire then sat back to watch as the flames danced and sparks flew up the chimney. On the unoccupied armchair on the other side of the fireplace was a plush pink cushion, heart-shaped, "R4M" picked out in sequins. Martin sighed as he pulled the ring on another can of lager.

Rosemarie stopped at the "For Sale" sign. Next door's cat, interrupted in his nocturnal patrol, swelled to twice his normal size, bared his fangs and spat like a pressure cooker, before making off across the gardens yowling in fear.

The disturbance drew Martin to the window. He peered out into the darkness. The meagre light from a street lamp several houses down reassured him that the dustbin lid was securely in place. He did not see the intricate pattern of ice crystals on the window pane made by a long exhalation of frozen breath.

Ruth was in the kitchen. Earlier that day she and Martin had completed a clear out of all the junk in the spare room and the loft. She had been amazed at the amount of clutter they had unearthed and felt very pleased with herself. The rubbish bags piled in the garden would need two journeys to the tip when it reopened. She opened the kitchen door and gazed with satisfaction at the row of bulging carriers lining the hallway ready for donation to local charity shops.

Ruth had rewarded herself with a relaxing bath and was wearing the very nice red velour dressing gown she had found neatly folded in the back of the airing cupboard, one of the very few items she considered worth keeping. The hall light flickered and grew dim and a sudden draught rattled the letterbox. Ruth shivered as she opened the sitting room door.

"I can't wait to get into our new place. These old houses are so chilly."

Martin took a swig of lager, but did not answer. Ruth perched on the arm of his chair and nibbled absentmindedly on the discarded cake.

"Is there any of that coffee liqueur left? Why is the telly off? You said you wanted to watch a film."

Ruth poured a generous measure of the creamy liquid, took a large swig and licked her lips.

"Lovely!"

She turned back to Martin who was staring in confusion at the red dressing gown.

"What's the matter?"

"Where did you find..?"

At that moment the belt slipped undone and the dressing gown opened, revealing an expanse of plump pink thigh and more besides. Martin's question remained unanswered.

After midnight and it seemed that all the world, apart from one restless soul, was sleeping. Martin, snug against Ruth's warm back, was snoring gently. In the sitting room a sudden icy blast burst from the chimney scattering glowing embers across the hearthrug and beyond. A half-burned log teetered on the edge of the grate then rolled across the floor and came to rest under the parched Christmas tree. Hungry flames were soon licking the brittle boughs. The nylon carpet, chosen all those years before by newly-wedded Rosemarie and Martin, began to smoulder. Swept by an invisible hand, the Christmas cards were tossed from the mantlepiece to be devoured alongside the heart-shaped cushion which shriveled and melted into nothing. Suffocating black smoke crept through the ground floor rooms and tiptoed up the staircase.

The fourth day of Christmas dawned bright. The church was bathed in morning sunshine; pigeons pecked and preened on the path leading to the lychgate. Over in Pear Tree Lane the emergency services had finally departed; a huddle of neighbours whispered in shock behind police tape.

Sue Maund

A Chance Meeting

Henry left the bank exactly at noon heading for the park for his usual place next to the aviary. In his fourties, he was tall, smartly dressed in his tailored suit and Brogues, carrying his leather briefcase and umbrella. It didn't look like he needed it today but it was his habit to carry it. He had a senior position in the bank and hoped to rise to bank manager in the near future, so status and dress was important to him.

Opening his briefcase he took out a carefully ironed handkerchief. Placing it on the bench he turned and sat down. Removing his metal lunchbox he opened it revealing crust-off sandwiches and a two finger Kit-Kat. His thermos flask was placed under his seat ready for when he needed it.

Ethel made her way towards Victoria Park and sat down on the same wooden bench to eat her lunch. Diving into her bag she brought out her Tupperware box and her little thermos flask. She was dressed in smart crimplene trousers with black matching Hush Puppies. Her pink twin set brought out the feint blush in her cheeks. The perfume of the flowers greeted her nostrils and she closed her eyes and sighed loudly.

"I'm so sorry", Henry said politely and he moved along the bench to give Ethel more room.

"What do you mean? she said confused. Did I do something to upset you? I really didn't mean to, y'know. I was just taking in the perfume of the flowers and sighing. Nothing more than that." She sighed again and started to collect her things.

"No, please Madam, said Henry. It is totally my fault. I thought, I mean, I misunderstood you. Please don't leave your seat and halt your lunch on my account". Henry looked embarrassed and needed to correct the situation. He waved his hand towards the bench indicating that Ethel should sit back down.

"If you're sure," she said meekly. "I don't mind y'know. I often get the wrong end of the stick".

Henry smiled at her warmly and she beamed back grateful for the chance to sit with him. "Please have one of my sandwiches as a peace offering for my mistake?" He watched her as she carefully took one from his lunch box.

"My name is Henry, may I ask you yours?" he said holding out his long fingered hand.

"Why thank you Henry. My name is Ethel and I can't complement you enough on your delicious sandwiches. I've never tasted any as good as these".

Henry beamed with pride at her words and suggested they share the Kit-Kat. Ethel talked about her work as a nurse coming to the park to relax before returning to the Royal for night duty.

Listening to Ethel talk, Henry began to realise how charming and genuine she was. He felt more comfortable with her than he had with any woman before. Looking at his watch, he realised he only had ten minutes before having to return to the bank.

"Ethel," he said shyly, "would you like to meet me here next week for lunch? I'll bring the sandwiches if you'll allow me and we can sit and enjoy the flowers together before you return to the hospital." Henry held his breathe as he waited anxiously for her reply.

"Why Henry, I would love to, and I'll bring the Kit-Kat" she replied giggling nervously. As they stood to go their separate ways a smile came over Henry's face. "Please take care of yourself Ethel. I will be looking forward to seeing you next Friday." Ethel blushed and smiled up at him. "I will too Henry".

As they parted, both had thoughts about their next meeting. Henry was already planning to make very special sandwiches and Ethel was thinking about buying a four-fingered Kit-Kat.

Bertie Bee's New Job

The excited bees sat down to breakfast whilst their parents tried to answer the questions being fired at them.

"How long will it take, Mama?"

"Do we fly far away?"

"How high can we go?"

"Enough, too many questions," said William Bee. "We all fly together to collect the pollen, then take the pollen to the hive for the worker bees. Now, is everyone ready?" he said, laughing out loud. Sheila Bee hurried the younger bees out of the house so they didn't get left behind. This was an important day for everyone.

Bertie was the biggest bee with the largest wings. He was able to fly the highest. He wanted to show his parents just how strong he was. Bertie flew from one flower to another and soon found his legs loaded with pollen. His parents took to the air and they all followed, flying to the hive to deliver their golden treasure. It was when they returned home Bertie felt unwell.

"Mama, my eyes are sore and itchy and my nose won't stop running." He sneezed several times. Sheila Bee felt his forehead and thought he might be going down with a bumble cold. She put him to bed and he fell asleep as soon as his bee head hit the pillow.

When Bertie awoke the next morning, he felt much better and tucked into his breakfast as usual. His father looked at him.

"I see you are feeling better today Bertie? That is good because we have a very busy day today."

"Yes father, I'm feeling much better, thank you. I'm going to fly even higher today and look for the best flowers." His father smiled and patted his back.

William Bee asked Bertie to fly high and direct them to the roses. The family followed Bertie as he found the way there. But when Bertie flew down to join his family his eyes became sore and itchy again and tears blurred his eyes. Sheila Bee stopped to look at him.

"Bertie Bee, are you feeling poorly again?"

"I don't know what is wrong with me Mama. My throat is sore and my eyes are leaking. I feel sick Mama."

"We'll go home together Bertie and see Dr. Ahmet." Bertie flew next to his mother but every time he sneezed, his little body shook so much, he bounced higher and higher and his mother had to pull him back down again. Sitting in the doctor's surgery Bertie held his handkerchief to his nose catching one sneeze after another.

"Oh dear, oh dear," came the voice of Dr. Ahmet. "It's been a long time since I've heard that type of sneezing. You'd better come into my office, Bertie Bee."

Bertie followed his mother into the examination room, sneezing loudly as he went, and sat down nervously. He wiped his eyes with his handkerchief before looking up at Dr Ahmet. His mother placed her hand on his knee to reassure him.

"Now Bertie, tell me when this started," the doctor asked. "

"How long have you been feeling so poorly?" His mother explained what they had done the last two days. Bertie turned to Dr. Ahmet.

"I was flying really high but when I flew down, my eyes started stinging and then they were leaking and then I sneezed and sneezed and sneezed," he said loudly. Dr. Ahmet examined Bertie's throat with his little wooden stick and hmm'd to himself, and nodded.

"Well Bertie, you have hay fever. I'm afraid that when you fly on the flowers, it affects you. I'm sure you'll grow out of it but, in the meantime I can give you some medicine to help you. Now Bertie, sometimes we can't always do the things we want to do, so I'm afraid, you will have to find another job. I know what a hard little worker you are and I'm sure you can do another job really well. Think about what you can do better than anyone else," he said winking at Bertie.

Bertie felt upset that he had let his family down. His mother made them a nice pot of tea as they waited for the family to return. Sitting around the dinner table they were all silent as they considered what Dr. Ahmet had said. That was until his sister, Becky Bee jumped up excitedly.

"I've got it!" she shouted. "I know exactly what Bertie can do! He is the only one who can fly high. I mean really, really high. That could be his new job and we can all follow him. That would be a very important job Bertie," she said feeling very proud of her big brother. Bertie looked at his sister and smiled thankfully at her.

The idea began to grow and the more Bertie thought about it, the more confident he felt about his new job. Looking up at his father eagerly, he smiled.

"I can do this father. I can fly higher than anyone and I can see for miles. I'll be able to show all the other bees where the best flowers are." William Bee patted Bertie on his back.

"Every bee has a job, Bertie, and I know you were worried that you'd let us down. But, you've found another job that you can do better than anyone else. We can call you Bertie Bee, Head Scout!"

His brothers and sisters all clapped and cheered as Bertie smiled the biggest smile. Bertie Bee, Head Scout sounded very special to him now.

Broken Heart

At some point the idea had come to her, not sure when, but her mind had been made up. She had reached her breaking point, unable to accept any further distress or pain. It was now time to end the agony that had gone on for far too long.

Laying the plastic sheet on the floor she carefully stepped onto it. Her coveralls and plastic covered boots would ensure all signs of her actions could be disposed of. The fridge had been prepared, as had the freezer, removing items, to make way for large odds and ends that couldn't be made smaller, well, not yet anyway. That would have to be done when she was on her own.

Black rubbish bags had been spread around her, their mouths greedily open ready to gobble up the evidence. Instruments she would need lay on a further plastic sheet, waiting eagerly, tempting her to get on with it. Did she finally have the guts to do it?

Breathing deeply, her mouth went dry as she stood trying to control her heartbeat. Her pulse quickened as the taste of vomit permeated her mouth. With shaking hands she picked up the first tool, while in the background, every magnified tick of the clock could be heard over the deafening quiet of the room.

Several hours later she released a deep sigh, stood back and closed the fridge door. Anxiety had given her a throbbing headache. Her neck and back felt worn and her muscles ached relentlessly. She hadn't anticipated the job being so tough, or taking as long as it did and certainly not as easy as seen on the TV, that's for sure. The amount of blood was another factor she hadn't accounted for, sticky, smelly, stuff. Thank God, she'd never have to do it again.

Her mind hurried her on, as she realised it was taking too long to clear away the mess, with splashes and drops everywhere. She seemed to be watching the clock continually, as time was running out. Once the evidence was hidden she would at last be able to relax. With the black plastic bags disposed of in the outdoor rubbish, she knew she could remove them once it was dark with no one around.

Hot soapy water mixed with pine disinfectant helped mask the smells, as she painfully washed down floors, walls and countertops. Taking one last glance at the clock, she gulped down a quick brandy, before heading for the shower, to remove any final evidence.

The family were expected for Sunday tea. She loved seeing them, and it was a family ritual they had upheld for ten years now. She'd missed them terribly when they'd moved out to go to University, both finding partners very quickly and having children.

She loved Bob, of course, but it was never the same as the children's love, and he was always so controlling. At least that would stop.

"Sylvie you must do it this way! No, you can't do that!" Well, he won't be telling her anymore, she'd made sure of that, hadn't she?

The sound of the doorbell brought her to her senses, as she heard the children's voices calling her through the letterbox. With an enormous smile on her face, she opened the door, as all the children fought for cuddles.

"Wow Nan! Your house smells good," said the oldest grandchild. With coats hung up, they settled down in the sitting room. Idle chatter meant everyone was catching up on the week's events. A casual remark about Bob not being there, made Sylvie cringe. Her heart raced as she made her way to the kitchen, to avoid anyone seeing her flushed. What had she done?

Quickly, she pulled it out of the fridge hoping no one would walk in. If she could get it out of the kitchen then no one would know. She'd be in the clear! Taking a second to gaze down she felt a small token of regret, but that thought was gone in a second. No, it was best to get rid of the evidence now, right this minute.

It only took three steps to the back door when all of a sudden it flew open as Buster raced in jumping up, his paws landing on her hips. Immediately her hands jolted and it flew through the air. His eyes flew to hers in shock. His lightening re-actions were as fast as hers were slow, catching it in mid-air. She looked at him in dread, paling immediately.

"I'm sorry Bob, so, so sorry. I just wanted to...." she trailed off.

"Umm," he said slowly looking down at his dripping hands holding two separate pieces. "When did you do this?" Slowly she lowered her hands and looked apologetically at him. "I...." her voice faltered."

"I never knew you had it in you, Sylvie." With that he lowered his hands, placing the pieces onto the plate. Looking up he smiled at her.

"Kids, you'd better come and see what your Mother has done." At Bob's voice everyone rushed into the kitchen to see what was happening. Bob pointed to the plate and laughed. "Take a look at that. Mum's finally made us a Halloween heart cake full of blood. And a broken one at that," he said, showing everyone the dripping blood on his hands. The whole family laughed and decided to celebrate by having a slice of Mum's very first Halloween cake.

The Croc Who Could Sing

Singing was all Winny the Croc wanted to do. She would sing all day long in the water, on the land, morning, noon and night.

In fact she sang so much, all the other crocodiles told her to be quiet or move away.

Winny was very sad about that, because she just wanted to make everyone happy.

Bear heard about this and said Winny could live with him, so she followed him to his cave.

She was very grateful for Bear's kindness, but it was a bit of a squeeze inside the cave, with his enormous body and her very long tail.

Bear told her she could sing, but, quietly, as he wanted to sleep.

Winny had never sung quietly before, but it was still too loud for Bear, so Winny had to leave the cave.

Snake slithered along and asked Winny why she was there. When she explained, Snake said she could live with him.

Winny followed Snake, but sadly the tree branches were too high for Winny, so she sang to Snake from the bottom of the tree trunk. It wasn't long before Snake dropped off.

Blackbird heard Winny singing beautifully.

"Please Winny, will you sing to my babies. They chirp all the time and are so noisy. I'd be so grateful if you can make them sleep."

Winny followed Blackbird to her nest and began to sing quietly to the fledglings. Gradually the noise of their chirping grew less and less and eventually stopped.

Winny felt so pleased with herself as she realised she could do something very special with her voice.

One by one the other animals came to ask her to sing to their animals to help them sleep.

It wasn't long before Winny became known as the Singing Nanny.

The Lion Who Wanted Curly Hair

Howard the Lion wanted curly hair. He had always wanted curly hair since he was a lion cub. Howard thought for a long time before deciding to ask Owl for advice. Owl was wise and knew the answers to so many things so Howard strolled up to the tree.

"Owl, are you there? I have a question for you," said Howard timidly. He didn't want the other animals to hear him. Owl looked down from his branch to see who was calling him.

"Is that you Howard? What is it I can help you with?"

"Can you tell me how I can get curly hair?" Howard whispered to Owl.

"What's that Howard, you want curly hair?" hooted Owl loudly.

Howard winced at Owls voice which had become very loud. He felt embarrassed about asking such a silly question.

"Yes Owl but please, talk quietly," Howard whispered to him.

"Nonsense, Howard. Go to the monkey house and ask Manna. She can give you curly hair."

Howard eagerly raced to the Monkey house to find Manna washing Snake and shinning her scales. Howard watched her as she worked slowly and carefully. When Manna had finished she saw Howard waiting.

"Can I help you Howard?" she asked." Howard looked at her shyly and whispered.

"Owl says you can give me curly hair."

"I can do that Howard. Take a seat and I'll be right back." Howard sat and waited for her to return. She came back in carrying a wicker basket which she put down on the table. Manna then washed Howard's hair for him. It was so relaxing that he closed his eyes dreaming of the beautiful curls he would have. Manna worked quickly putting in fir cones all over his hair to dry. An hour later she woke him as he had dropped off to sleep.

"Wake up Howard, your hair is finished now," said Manna proudly.

Opening his eyes Howard smiled broadly as Manna gave him a mirror to see his new hair. Beautiful shiny curls hung down through his mane making him look magnificent and regal. Howard was ecstatic at his new look.

"Thank you Manna. I love my curls," said Howard gratefully.

As he left Manna's house he walked taller than he ever had done before. Howard really did look like the King of the Jungle now.

The Tortoise Who Thought He Could Race

Tommy Tortoise had ambitions on winning the annual race. He knew he had short legs and he knew they were slow. None of the other animals had to carry their house on their back all day long. Did they not realise how heavy it was? It was no wonder he was tired all of the time.

Tommy had to think of a way to solve his problem. He couldn't take his house off or grow his legs longer, or, could he? He thought very hard and knew just who to ask. So off he went to visit Octopus. Tommy thought that as Octopus had 8 legs, surely he could lend him a couple or 4. Octopus was very busy knitting a jumper and studied Tommy as he sat in the chair.

"I'm so sorry Tommy, I am too busy today. I think you should go to see Fox and ask him for some advice." Fox listened to Tommy's problem and thought hard for a minute.

"I do have an idea or three, Tommy. Come back here tomorrow and let's see what I can do." Tommy returned eagerly the next day and saw Fox had a selection of items laid out on the floor.

"Let's try these to see how you get on." First of all Fox handed Tommy a pair of roller skates but as soon as he put them on Tommy fell over.

"They won't do Tommy. How about this one then?" Fox gave him a bicycle. Tommy sat on the saddle and toppled over sideways.

"No said Fox shaking his head, that won't do at all. You had better try this scooter then."

Tommy held onto the handle bars and put one foot on the scooter and pushed off with his other foot. Before he knew it he was scooting down the road as fast as can be.

"Wheeee," cried Tommy. "I'm going so fast. This is great. Now I can race on this scooter." Fox looked on as Tommy scooted faster and faster. Fox felt extremely pleased with himself. It had had not been easy to help solve Tommy's problem.

When race day came all the animals lined up ready for the gun. 'BANG! The gun went off.

Tommy wasn't the quickest to start but slowly he managed to increase his speed. He overtook hedgehog and snake, then mouse and rabbit. Finally he overtook hare who was busy posing for photos. Hare hadn't even noticed Tommy going past. Tommy was having so much fun on the scooter before he knew it he'd reached the red ribbon to win the race. When he held up the trophy with red ribbon on the handle for his photograph to be taken, he shouted out.

"Wait," he cried, "I need my friend here too. Without fox I wouldn't have won the race. Thank you Fox, for being such a good friend," said Tommy."

The photographer took their photo as Fox and Tommy laughed and ate the winning jelly beans they had found inside the trophy.